DEATH EN VOYAGE

BY THE SAME AUTHOR:

THE MURDERS AT IMPASSE LOUVAIN

THE MONTERANT AFFAIR

THE DEATH OF ABBÉ DIDIER

THE MONTMARTRE MURDERS

CRIME WITHOUT PASSION

RICHARD GRAYSON

St. Martin's Press
New York

Library of Congress Cataloging in Publication Data

Grayson, Richard.
Death en voyage.

I. Title.
PR6057.R55D38 1986 823'.914 86-1824
ISBN 0-312-18606-1

First published in Great Britain by Victor Gollancz Ltd.

First U.S. Edition

10 9 8 7 6 5 4 3 2 1

DEATH EN VOYAGE

1

THE CONCIERGE IN his red frock coat and black trousers greeted Gautier with the same dignified courtesy that he would show to the Russian grand dukes, English milords and Spanish grandees who often patronized the Hotel Cheltenham. He was resolutely, almost ostentatiously, unperturbed. In the faces and the manner of the other members of the hotel staff—the pages, the lift boy and the chambermaids—one could see the suppressed excitement, the fearful fascination which a sudden and unexpected appearance of death always provokes. The concierge, on the other hand, knew it was his responsibility to set an example and to show that the order and discipline of his hotel could not be disrupted, even by such a deplorable incident as a murder.

'I will take you up myself, Inspector,' he said and Gautier recognized that a compliment was intended.

As they walked up the main staircase to the second floor, he was glad that they had not taken the elevator which moved ponderously up and down the centre of the hotel in its iron cage, for the concierge would not wish to discuss the murder in front of any guests who might be riding in the elevator nor even in front of the lift boy. All Gautier knew were the facts which had been reported to the Sûreté. An Englishwoman had been found murdered in her suite at the Hotel Cheltenham in Rue du Faubourg St. Honoré.

'Is the dead woman known to you?' he asked the concierge.

'Lady Dorothy? Certainly, Monsieur l'Inspecteur. She has been a regular guest for six or seven years or more. Lady Dorothy always stayed with us whenever she visited Paris.'

'Was she travelling alone?'

'No, with her companion, a Miss Mary Newbolt. It was Miss Newbolt who found Lady Dorothy dead in her suite this morning.'

'Her husband was not with her?'

'Lady Dorothy was not married,' the concierge replied, slipping easily into the past tense, 'but she was of noble birth. The late Earl of Tain was her brother.'

He went on to mention the names of some of Lady Dorothy's other relatives, more distant than her brother but equally well born. The concierge was knowledgeable about genealogy, not only because it was useful to him in his profession, and his favourite reading was the *Almanach de Gotha*, which listed Europe's noble families and traced their ancestry.

'Do you know what time the lady's death was discovered?' Gautier asked.

'Not long after I came on duty. It must have been at about twenty minutes past seven. Miss Newbolt rang for one of the chambermaids and sent the girl to fetch me at once.'

A uniformed policeman who had been called in when the murder had been discovered, was standing outside the door to which the concierge led Gautier. Inside, in the drawing-room of the suite, a doctor was kneeling over the body of a woman. He had just completed his examination and stood up, shutting his bag as he did so. A woman of about thirty stood watching him and a maid with her apron held up to her face was sobbing quietly in a corner of the room. Gautier shook hands with the doctor, whom he had met before, and was about to offer his hand to the young woman but she merely nodded when the doctor introduced him. He remembered then that the English were supposed to have all sorts of taboos and social protocol and that in any case they were less enthusiastic about shaking hands than the French.

'Unfortunately, there was nothing I could do for the lady, Inspector,' the doctor said. 'She was already dead when I arrived.'

Gautier looked at the body which lay not in an untidy sprawl as one might have expected but neatly, the limbs straight, almost as though in repose. Blood had gushed from a wound below the left breast, staining the black silk dress, and a blood-stained knife lay on the floor beside the body. Lady Dorothy had been a tall, slim woman and the chief feature of her face was a long, curved nose which made the mouth seem small and pinched. Her long grey hair lay loosely around her head and shoulders.

When the doctor left the room, Gautier went with him and the concierge into the corridor outside. There he asked the doctor, 'Are you able to say at what time the lady was killed?'

'Not too many hours ago. There are no signs of rigor mortis yet.'

'Then since she was dressed in day clothes we might conclude that it was this morning.'

'I would think so, yes. We will arrange for her body to be taken to the mortuary and properly examined. Then perhaps we may know more.'

Gautier turned towards the concierge. 'Did you say that the lady's companion found the body?'

'So I understand.'

'Was she sharing the suite with her employer?'

'No. She has a bedroom on the fifth floor. And the girl you saw in the corner of the room is Lady Dorothy's personal maid. She too was travelling with her and has a room in the servants' quarters.'

Gautier knew it was not unusual for wealthy people to take their servants with them when they travelled. A voyage to a country other than their own became an expedition with maids, valets, innumerable trunks and hat boxes. As a spinster, though, Lady Dorothy would not have needed such an elaborate retinue.

'Does the companion speak French?'

'Yes, Inspector. Better French than poor Lady Dorothy did.'

After the doctor and the concierge had left, Gautier returned to the drawing-room of the suite. Miss Newbolt was still standing where she had been while the doctor was examining Lady Dorothy's body. She seemed calm and composed, unaffected as far as one could tell by the death of her employer, but then she would be accustomed, Gautier supposed, to being no more than a passive onlooker, waiting in attendance until her services or her opinions were requested.

'I wonder, Mademoiselle,' he said to her, 'if I might ask for your assistance.'

'In what way?'

'Would you be so kind as to tell me what you know of this most unfortunate affair?'

'Of course, Inspector, but could I first prevail on your patience?'

'Mademoiselle?'

'I would like to return to my room to wash and change my clothes.'

She held out her hands, showing that the palms and fingers were smeared with dried blood and Gautier realized then why she had not offered to shake hands with him. The plain grey dress which she wore was also stained with blood at the sleeves and on the skirt.

'I am desolate, Mademoiselle, for not noticing your predicament earlier. You must go and change, that goes without saying. Go to your room and I will send a message telling you where to meet me. It would be better if we were not to talk in this room.'

'Why not?'

Gautier shrugged his shoulders. 'Just police procedure. The room must be carefully examined for anything which might help us discover who killed Lady Dorothy. The management will find another room in the hotel where we can talk.'

She left the room without making any further comment. When she had gone, Gautier looked at the body of the Englishwoman once again. It lay on a line between a writing bureau and the door leading from the drawing-room into the corridor. On the bureau itself he found several sheets of notepaper, an inkwell and a pen. The top sheet of paper was half covered in a sprawling handwriting and another sheet, completely covered in the same writing, had been pushed on one side. Recognizing that the words were English, a language he scarcely knew at all, he folded the two sheets of paper and put them away in his pocket.

Two more doors led off the drawing-room, one into a large bedroom and the other into a surprising luxury, a bathroom. Few homes in Paris had bathrooms and most people took their baths in zinc tubs which were taken to their bedrooms and filled with hot water from jugs by chambermaids. Gautier supposed that bathrooms must have been recently installed at the Hotel Cheltenham and then only in the more expensive suites.

On the dressing-table in the bedroom he noticed two photographs in silver frames, one a faded wedding portrait of a young man in the uniform of a guards' regiment, with a pretty but anaemic girl on his arm, and the other of an extraordinarily beautiful young woman. None of the drawers in either the dressing-table or a chest of drawers were open and Gautier could see no signs of the disorder one would have expected if robbery had been the motive for the Englishwoman's murder.

Returning to the drawing-room he found that his principal assistant, Surat, had arrived from the Sûreté. Surat was a model police officer, loyal, courageous and dedicated to his work, but he had been passed over for promotion and at his age was unlikely to be given it now.

Gautier explained to him as concisely as he could the circumstances of Lady Dorothy's murder. Then he asked, 'Did you bring any men with you?'

'Yes, patron, two. They are in the corridor outside.'

'Good. Then the three of you please search all the rooms of this suite as meticulously as you can. See if you can find anything, anything at all, which will explain why this woman came to be stabbed. When you have finished, seal the doors in the usual way and put a notice up forbidding anyone to enter.'

'Anything more?'

'Yes. Afterwards make enquiries among the hotel staff; the chambermaids, the waiters, everyone. Find out if any strangers were seen about the hotel this morning. If the Englishwoman was killed by an intruder someone may have noticed him in the corridors or on the stairs. Speak to everyone, but do it discreetly. We do not want to disturb or alarm the other guests.'

Leaving Surat to start searching the room, Gautier went downstairs to see the hotel manager. He told him of the arrangements which were being made to take the murdered woman's body to the mortuary and agreed to his request that this should be done through a side door of the hotel, used by the staff and out of sight of other guests. In return, the manager put another room on the second floor at Gautier's disposal, where he could interview Miss Newbolt and also any members of the hotel staff who might come forward with information. Then he went back to Lady Dorothy's suite to see how the search was progressing.

'Have you found anything to suggest why the Englishwoman was murdered?' he asked Surat.

'Not yet. There are no signs whatsoever of a robber having been in here. If anything was stolen then whoever it was must have come knowing exactly what he wanted and where it was hidden. Nothing, no papers or any of her clothes have been disturbed. The place is almost too tidy.'

'Lady Dorothy had a maid travelling with her.'

'We found one thing which it seemed rather strange that a spinster should be taking with her on her travels. A man's cigarette case. It was in a drawer of the dressing-table.'

The cigarette case was in a chamois leather pouch and Surat showed it to Gautier. It was a silver case but in no way unusual and in all probability, Gautier decided, not expensive. The outside of the case was plain but on the inside he found an inscription.

A Mon Bien Aimé

Immediately below the inscription was an engraving of a single rosebud.

When Miss Newbolt came into the drawing-room of another suite on the second floor where Gautier was waiting, she was wearing a grey dress identical as far as one could tell to the one she had been wearing earlier, except for the blood stains. The dress was simply cut and without embellishment of any kind, a style in keeping with the way she had drawn her light brown hair back and tied it in a bun behind her neck. Her face, if one looked at the features singly, was not unattractive, but one might have believed that she had taken some pains to disguise the fact.

Guessing that she would not have taken breakfast that morning, Gautier had ordered coffee and fresh bread to be brought to the room and when she arrived he offered it to her. Miss Newbolt seemed surprised.

'That's most considerate of you, Inspector. Thank you, I'll take a cup of coffee, nothing more.'

He poured the coffee and handed it to her. She glanced at him over the cup as she raised it to her lips; a wary look, as though she suspected the motives behind his considerate gesture.

'I understand that it was you who found Lady Dorothy's body.'

'Yes, I did.'

'May I ask how that came about?'

'I came down to the suite and when I saw that the door to the corridor was open I realized something must be wrong. She was lying on the floor just where you saw her later. I pulled the knife out but it was too late. She was already dead.'

'She seems to have been writing a letter when she was disturbed.'

'Lady Dorothy was always an early riser. She would get up at seven and read or write letters till her maid came down at seven forty-five to do her hair. I would join her for breakfast at eight every morning.'

'But you came down earlier today?'

'Yes. Soon after seven.'

'Why was that?'

'Do you know, I'm not sure.' Miss Newbolt's reply was immediate and Gautier wondered if she had rehearsed an answer to a question she had been expecting. 'I woke suddenly and began to wonder whether Lady Dorothy was all right. So I came down to see. It sounds ridiculous, I know, but I had a kind of premonition that she might be in danger.'

In Gautier's experience people often claimed to have had premonitions of disaster after disaster had struck, but if they had they seldom acted on them. He decided not to press the matter and instead he changed the line of questioning. 'Can you think of any reason why Lady Dorothy should have been murdered?'

'Robbery, I suppose.'

'Did she keep anything of any special value in her room? Jewellery?'

'She had brought very little with her; only a gold ring with the family coat of arms and a gold and sapphire locket in which she carried a miniature portrait of her brother as a boy.'

'Where would she have kept those?'

'She probably just put them on the dressing-table when she took them off. Lady Dorothy was very careless. But she also had a sum of money with her.'

'Did she always carry a large sum of cash?'

'No, but yesterday afternoon she called at a bank and drew on a letter of credit. I don't know what amount she drew but I believe it was substantial.'

'Have you any idea why she needed the money?' Gautier asked. 'For travelling expenses?'

'I wouldn't think so. When we travelled abroad Lady Dorothy brought letters of credit with her and drew just enough money to pay the bills immediately before we left each place that we visited.'

'She was a regular traveller then?'

'Yes. She always came to the Continent every year.'

'Tell me about these voyages.'

Lady Dorothy's travels in Europe, Miss Newbolt told Gautier, always followed the same pattern and generally an identical itinerary. From London she would come by train and steamer to Paris where she would usually spend a week. This gave her time not only to visit the art galleries and museums and churches but to have fittings with Paquin and Worth. From Paris she and Miss Newbolt would go overland first to Florence and then, for a very brief stay, to Venice. Much though she loved the beauty of Venice, Lady Dorothy would never spend more than a couple of days there, distrusting the smells from the canals and believing they might infect her with diphtheria. After Venice came Vienna and then two weeks taking the waters in Baden-Baden. Finally they would return to Paris, spending just enough time there to pick up the dresses that had been made for Lady Dorothy before heading for the welcoming cliffs of Dover.

'Lady Dorothy has been making the same tour for several years,' Miss Newbolt concluded. 'And for the last five I've been her travelling companion.'

Although she had described Lady Dorothy's travels in some detail, Gautier thought he detected a reticence in her manner, as though she had something more to tell but which she felt she should not volunteer. He asked her, 'So this was no different from any of your other voyages with your employer?'

'It differed in two respects,' Miss Newbolt admitted with a show of reluctance. 'Lady Dorothy's travels on the Continent were always planned meticulously. New hats and gloves were bought for the voyage, reservations made well in advance at her usual hotels, letters of instructions sent to travel agents and couriers. Nothing was ever left to chance. But this time it was different. I was only told we were coming just over a week ago.'

'And can you think of any reason for that?'

'None.'

'You said this voyage was different from the others in two respects. What was the second difference?'

Miss Newbolt smiled; a tiny smile without pleasure or humour. 'It was different, Inspector, because we both knew it was to be the last voyage I would make with her.'

'Why was that?'

'I was to leave her employment in one month's time.'

'Of your own volition?'

Miss Newbolt hesitated before she answered the question but only for an instant. 'Yes.' She looked at Gautier defiantly before she went on: 'I'm sure you have been wondering, Inspector, why Lady Dorothy's death has left me unmoved. You have seen no tears, no distress.'

'English people are recognized to be less emotional than we French. They are adept at keeping—how do you call it—the stiff upper lip.'

'No doubt,' Miss Newbolt said drily. 'But I have good reason for my lack of emotion. I am not distressed nor even sorry that Lady Dorothy is dead. You see I hated the woman.'

2

'THIS IS REALLY most regrettable, Gautier, most regrettable!'

Courtrand, Director-General of the Sûreté, was walking up and down his office, an unmistakable sign of his indignation. In the normal way he preferred to remain seated when any of his subordinates reported to him, so that his short stature and corpulence were concealed by his vast desk.

'What will the British think?' he continued. 'That we cannot protect our distinguished visitors? This unfortunate affair could sour the good relationship between our two countries, which some of us have worked so hard to foster.'

Without being in any way cynical, Gautier understood the reasons for Courtrand's concern. Not many months previously, the director-general had been decorated by the British Government with the Order of the British Empire for the part he had played in foiling an attempt to assassinate Edward VII when the king was enjoying himself with a former mistress in a box at the opera while on a private visit to Paris. Since that time Courtrand appeared to have convinced himself that the fragile Entente Cordiale recently formed between Britain and France was largely of his making.

'It's monstrous!' Courtrand exclaimed. 'How did an intruder get into the lady's room undetected? Hotels of good standing must have the means to protect their guests from voyous and ruffians off the streets. I don't understand how this happened.'

'We cannot be sure that Lady Dorothy was stabbed by an intruder,' Gautier replied.

'Why do you say that?'

'So far as one can tell nothing was stolen from the lady's room. She may have had a large sum of money with her but that is only hearsay. We don't know for certain.'

'Who found the body? A hotel servant?'

'No. Lady Dorothy's companion.'

'Companion? What companion?'

When, on returning to Sûreté headquarters, Gautier had reported to Courtrand, he had told him only the facts of Lady Dorothy's murder. Now he briefly described the circumstances of the killing and how Miss Newbolt had found the body. He also told Courtrand of the blood he had seen on Miss Newbolt's hands and on her dress.

'Then the companion might have killed her!' Courtrand exclaimed and as he thought about the idea it began to appeal to him. 'If that is the case we need not be concerned. We French cannot be blamed.'

'Possibly.'

'Have you brought the woman here for further questioning?'

'No, Monsieur.'

'Mother of God, why not, Gautier? You have enough grounds for detaining her for questioning at least.'

'I felt we should proceed more circumspectly. What if we were to establish that she was not involved in her employer's death, that Lady Dorothy had after all been stabbed by a thief? Might not the Sûreté be accused of harassing the woman? She is employed by important people.'

'You may be right.' Courtrand nodded thoughtfully.

'I decided it was best to leave her undisturbed this morning, so that she can telegraph the dead woman's relatives and contact the British Embassy here. And even if she should be guilty of killing her mistress she cannot flee. Where would she go?'

'But you'll resume your questioning of her this afternoon?'

'Yes, Monsieur. I told her to make herself available.'

'Good and when you do, impound her passport. In the meantime make out a full report on the affair, Gautier. As you know, the Prefect of Police is not in Paris at the present time, but the Minister of Justice must be informed in case there are diplomatic repercussions.'

Gautier left the room feeling rather pleased with the way he had handled Courtrand. Too often his interviews with the director-general became no more than a string of complaints about the way in which Gautier was conducting a case and often they ended in a rebuke. Now, like the other senior inspectors of the Sûreté, he found he could make life easier for himself by playing on the man's weaknesses. Courtrand's appointment as head of the Sûreté had been, as most senior public posts were, a piece of political patronage, a reward for some service he had done for a person of importance. Since he had been appointed, Courtrand, either through gratitude or in the hope of further advancement, had been obsequiously loyal to all important people, not only government ministers and officials senior to himself, but aristocrats, bankers and the wealthy bourgeois families. He looked after their interests and used his position at the Sûreté to shelter them, as far as he possibly could, from trouble or inconvenience. Gautier had found that if one could convince Courtrand that a course of action would work to the advantage of wealthy or important people in society then he would approve it.

Upstairs in his office he found lying on his desk the two sheets of notepaper he had taken from the writing bureau in Lady Dorothy's suite and a French translation of what she had written, which had been made in the Sûreté at his request. It read:

Dear Alice,

I am making progress but what depresses me is that the truth may very well be exactly what you and I feared. I met Monsieur J-J. T. by arrangement at the Salle Delacroix yesterday afternoon. My dear, I had forgotten what an odious creature he is! But he is the best man to help us and will do so for a consideration of course. I suspect he is in financial straits. He assured me that that place to which the money was being sent for all those years, the Hotel de Lascombes, is one of those places where men go to meet men. Quite disgusting! Of course I cannot possibly go there myself so T. said he would go there at once and make enquiries about the mysterious Monsieur D. I fear the worst. Poor Kate!

I took the cigarette case to a jeweller near the hotel, but he told me it would be impossible to trace it. It seems that it is of poor quality, as is the engraving, and the jeweller said there must be at least 50 shops in the poorer parts of Paris where it might have been bought.

Newbolt has been difficult and moody, which is not surprising, I suppose. It might have been better to have sent her packing as soon as I dismissed her, but with her fluent French she is useful on a voyage like mine. She has said nothing about the packet and that's another worry. God knows what was . . .

Thoughtfully, Gautier put the letter and the translation away in a drawer of his desk alongside the cigarette case which he had brought away with him from the Hotel Cheltenham. He had another question now to ask Miss Newbolt when she came to the Sûreté that afternoon. She would have to explain to him why she had been lying.

As he crossed the Seine and strolled along Boulevard St. Michel, Gautier found himself wondering about English cafés. They would have cafés in England, of course, but would they in any way resemble the Café Corneille? In France the café was an institution, a place where men went for companionship and conversation, to listen to gossip and laugh at rumours, but also to argue light-heartedly, wittily, passionately. The English, he had heard, had gentlemen's clubs, oases where men of wealth and breeding could find refuge from their women, but in France there were cafés to cater for everyone; for bankers and lawyers and actors and diamond merchants and candle makers. Possibly the only group of men who did not have a café where they could count on finding others in the same métier were policemen, and Gautier was secretly proud to have found one where he was accepted as an equal by the other habitués and regarded by many of them as a friend.

When he reached the Café Corneille that day, most of the small clique whom he met when he went there were already seated at their usual table: an elderly lawyer, a brilliant young judge who was making a name for himself in politics, Froissart the bookseller and his closest friend, Duthrey, a journalist who worked for *Figaro*.

Although most of the group were men of catholic tastes, interested in culture and in life, that day they were talking politics. French society was passing through a phase of cynical pessimism about politics and politicians at that time. A series of scandals during the past twenty years had eroded what little confidence the French had ever felt in the honesty and integrity of those who governed them. A President of the Republic, Jules Grévy, had been forced to resign when it was discovered that his son-in-law was selling decorations, including the coveted Légion d'Honneur. Not long afterwards, the bankruptcy of the company which was building the Panama Canal, with the loss of 150 million francs of investors' money, had brought the Government down and put several politicians on trial. A lesser but more salacious scandal was the Flower Girl Affair, when a duke from one of France's oldest families, together with another prominent member of society, had been imprisoned for procuring schoolgirls for their sexual orgies. Then had come the aftermath of the court martial of Dreyfus, with accusations of forgery and collusion, which had divided France into two bitter camps.

'Clemenceau is not to be trusted,' Duthrey remarked as Gautier took his seat at the table.

'Never!' the elderly lawyer agreed. 'Déroulède was right. Clemenceau was as implicated in the Panama débâcle as any of those who went to jail.'

'There was no evidence that he had lined his pockets from Panama,' the young judge pointed out. 'One should not condemn the man just for his radical views.'

'I don't,' the lawyer replied, 'but traitors should be unmasked. Clemenceau is a secret agent for England.'

'That's absurd!'

'Has he not always attacked any government policy that could be considered as hostile to England?'

'We need the friendship of England,' Froissart observed. 'Now that Russia has shown herself to be a broken reed, we have no friends in Europe.'

The disastrous defeat sustained by Russia in her short, dramatic war with Japan was still fresh in the minds of the French. The blunders and military incompetence which caused the débâcle had been a joke in Paris. The press had taken delight in describing how drunken naval officers of the Tsar's fleet, as it set out through the North Sea for Japan, had fired on British fishing vessels, imagining them to be Japanese torpedo boats lying in wait for them.

'Clemenceau is like his English paymasters,' the lawyer persisted. 'Hypocritical and treacherous.'

'Come, gentlemen! Now Victoria is dead we should forget our anglophobia.'

'The man's a cad! He treated his wife shamefully.' Duthrey, since he had written a series of articles on family life in France, was always quick to defend the sanctity of marriage.

Gautier listened to the friendly argument without taking sides. Then, as it petered out, he took advantage of a pause in the conversation to ask a question of his own. 'Can anyone imagine who a Monsieur J-J. T. might be?'

'Is this a guessing game?' Froissart demanded.

'It will not be as innocent as that,' Duthrey replied.

'Give us another clue.'

'Expecting a policeman to give away a clue is like asking a politician to give an honest opinion,' Gautier replied.

'Are we talking of a politician?'

'Possibly, but I would think not. More probably someone with an interest in art.'

'You know nothing more of him?'

'He may mix with pédés.'

'Homosexuals!' Froissart exclaimed. 'Then surely you must be talking of Jean-Jacques Touraine.'

'Of course! Who else?'

'He doesn't know of the infamous Touraine! But then he's too young,' Duthrey teased. 'We keep forgetting how young you are, Gautier.'

'Touraine is a poet,' Froissart explained, 'besides being a journalist. Ten years ago everyone in Parisian literary circles would know of him. And if they did not it was no fault of Touraine's.'

Between them Gautier's friends sketched a verbal portrait of Jean-Jacques Touraine. The man had been a poseur, they said, always drawing attention to himself. No affectation was too petty, no vice too monstrous for him to claim that he indulged in it. A writer of undoubted talent, he had wasted his gifts on maliciously witty chronicles of life in Paris, seeking to establish his reputation, it seemed, by destroying those of other people. And if any other writer wrote even a lukewarm review of one of his own volumes of verse, he would take his revenge with a savage attack on the writer. In spite of his malice and in spite of his poses, he had been accepted by Paris society and invited to the salons of many of the most fashionable hostesses.

'Why do you all speak of him in the past tense?' Gautier asked. 'The man isn't dead.'

'He's not dead,' the lawyer replied. 'But his reputation is. It was killed by Oscar Wilde.'

Gautier understood what he meant. Before the trial and imprisonment of Wilde, homosexuals were tolerated in French society. To have a self-professed homosexual or two in one's salon was even considered smart by the more daring hostesses of the gratin or upper crust, but the downfall and disgrace of Wilde had brought a swift reaction. Pédérastes were ostracized and people even began complaining that homosexuality was corrupting the masculinity of France and so damaging her capacity to win the war of revenge against Germany which national pride demanded.

'At least Touraine had the sense not to attack Clemenceau,' Duthrey said and Gautier realized that his friend wished to change the subject of the conversation.

'Yes. They say Clemenceau is deadly with the pistol,' he said.

'As deadly with the pistol at dawn as he is with his tongue in debate.' The young judge pulled a face because he had not long since been a victim of Clemenceau's scorn in the Chamber of Deputies.

The conversation switched back to politics again and Gautier felt guilty for having mentioned, even indirectly, a subject connected with police work. In times of political unrest the authorities had been known to plant spies and agents provocateurs in cafés and it was a flattering proof of his friends' belief in Gautier's integrity that they had accepted him into their circle. And there was a tacit understanding that neither they nor he would make any reference to the work he might be doing for the Sûreté.

Some time later, when Duthrey left the café to return home for the lunch his wife would have ready, Gautier walked a little way with him along Boulevard St. Germain.

'Touraine still writes,' Duthrey remarked. 'We published an article by him in *Figaro* only today.'

'Yes? On what subject?'

'The exhibition of surrealist art at the Salle Delacroix. I cannot imagine why anyone should be interested in the weird daubs and drink-sodden fantasies of those clowns up on the Butte.' Duthrey paused and then he added: 'They tell me Touraine lives in squalid rooms near the Gare du Nord. Our office would have his address.'

3

TOURAINE'S ROOMS WERE in a dreary part of Paris but the rooms themselves were not as squalid as Duthrey's remark might have led one to expect. The concierge directed Gautier to the third floor of the narrow house and he found Touraine in a large room which combined the functions of drawing-room, dining-room and study but which, although overcrowded with heavy furniture, paintings and ornaments, was comfortable and inviting, the kind of room which one would expect a good bourgeois mother to provide for her family.

'What brings you here, Inspector?' Touraine asked when Gautier had explained who he was.

He was a man almost large enough to be called gross, with soft features and plump hands on which he wore several ornate rings. Instead of adding masculinity to his face, the small, pointed moustache he had grown looked faintly absurd, as though it had been stuck on above his lip as part of a comic disguise. Over the fireplace of the room hung a portrait in oils of a heavy, dark-haired woman and one could tell by the very strong facial resemblance that she must be the poet's mother.

'You may not be aware, Monsieur,' Gautier replied, 'that Lady Dorothy Strathy is dead. She was murdered this morning in her hotel room.'

One could see at once that Touraine had not heard of Lady Dorothy's murder, but he concealed his surprise and paused only long enough to phrase a neutral reply. 'How does that affect me, may I ask?'

'You knew the lady, I believe.'

'Only slightly. I met her some years ago when I was staying with friends in London.'

'And again by appointment at the Salle Delacroix during her present visit to Paris.'

Alarm flared in Touraine's eyes, but he kept his voice under control as he replied; 'You must be mistaken, Inspector.'

'The lady left a half-finished letter which she had been writing and in which she mentioned meeting you.'

'In that case I admit we did meet at the exhibition but I promised Lady Dorothy I would tell no one of it.'

'Why was that?'

'She came to me for information on a matter which she found embarrassing.'

'About the Hotel de Lascombes, was it not?'

'Inspector, this was a private matter!' Touraine began to bluster. 'You had no right to read the lady's letter.'

'You do not seem to understand, Monsieur. She is dead. She was brutally stabbed.' Some people when questioned by the police, Gautier knew, responded better to rougher treatment. 'You would be well advised to answer my questions now for that may save you undergoing a more searching examination later.'

'All I told Lady Dorothy,' Touraine gave in petulantly, 'was that the Hotel de Lascombes is a male brothel. You know that as well as I do.'

'And you agreed to carry out a small commission for her. Was that to be at the hotel as well?'

'I said I would make some discreet enquiries on the lady's behalf.'

'What enquiries?'

'I don't know. She was going to give me precise instructions later.'

There was no doubt in Gautier's mind that Touraine was lying and he realized that the man was not going to be bullied or frightened into saying what he knew for the time being at least. During the years he had spent at the Sûreté, he had learnt to recognize the difference between a deliberate lie and a stubborn determination to conceal information. He was not irritated by Touraine's obstinacy nor even curious to know the reason for it. The truth would come out in due course. As they were talking he had become aware of a curious smell in the room, a combination of odours which he identified only slowly as the heavy, cloying scent of a popular woman's perfume which almost disguised, as no doubt it was meant to do, the pungent smell of ether. He remembered that Touraine had the reputation of being an éthéromane. The man's resistance to questioning might well weaken when the effects of any ether he had inhaled had evaporated.

'I shall not pretend, Monsieur Touraine,' he said, 'that the answers you have given me are satisfactory. I shall return and speak with you again tomorrow.'

'As you please, but it would suit me better to come to the Sûreté.'

The answer intrigued Gautier. Most people shrank instinctively from the prospect of visiting the headquarters of the Sûreté on Quai des Orfèvres. He said, 'That may not be convenient, Monsieur.'

'You have no right to visit my home uninvited.' Touraine began to grow agitated. 'I insist on being questioned at the Sûreté or if you prefer at the Ministry of Justice.'

'I find your attitude disturbing, Monsieur. Can it be that you are thinking of leaving Paris?'

'Certainly not!'

Gautier ignored the denial, sensing that if he persisted in the line he was taking he would soon find out the reason for Touraine's agitation. 'In that case it may be necessary for me to put a uniformed policeman on guard outside the building.'

'No! I forbid it! I shall not allow you to. Do you understand that?' Touraine shouted. Then, seeing that his protests were making no impression on Gautier, he changed his tactics. 'Inspector, I implore you! My old mother is coming to spend a few days with me. She will be arriving from our home in Brittany this evening. Can you imagine how upset and frightened she would be to find the police here, to know that I was under surveillance?'

Without thinking, Gautier glanced at the portrait of the woman which hung above the fireplace. He recalled reading of a theory that boys whose childhood was dominated by an obsession for their mothers often grew up to be either promiscuous in their dealings with women or to be homosexuals. Touraine's concern was so transparently genuine that he felt a sympathy for the man.

'All right, Monsieur. I have no wish to cause your mother pain.

Please be kind enough to present yourself at my office tomorrow morning at ten o'clock.'

As he was leaving the room, he paused by the door and looked at the poet. 'Some money which Lady Dorothy drew from a bank yesterday is missing. If you know anything about it, Monsieur, you would do better to tell me now.'

Touraine's heavy cheeks flushed with anger but with an effort he managed to keep his temper in check. He said stiffly: 'I know nothing of any money, Inspector. You have my assurance that Lady Dorothy gave me none.'

'Gautier, did I not instruct you to write me a full report on this affair of the English milady?'

'Yes, Monsieur, you did.'

'Then why have you not done so?'

'I finished the report this morning and gave it to your secretary.'

Courtrand fought back his irritation and then, to work off some of his frustration, yelled loudly for his secretary who worked in a tiny office next to his own. Corbin, a small, self-effacing man, precise and slow and thorough, a typical petit fonctionnaire, came in at his own pace and stared at Courtrand solemnly.

'What have you done with Gautier's report?' Courtrand demanded.

'I sent it immediately to the Minister of Justice as you instructed me to, Monsieur.'

'Did you not have a copy made for me?'

'No, Monsieur. You said nothing about a copy and as you know copies take time to prepare. Even now, using those infernal writing machines, the clerks downstairs can take an hour or more to copy a report. I understood you to say that the Minister should have the report with all speed.'

Courtrand waved the man away and buried his face in his hands with exaggerated despair. He had long ago convinced himself that all those who worked under him were incompetent and he enjoyed an opportunity of reminding himself and others of this fact. When Corbin had left the room he asked Gautier, 'Was there anything in your report which you did not mention to me this morning?'

'Nothing of any consequence, Monsieur.'

'Are you certain? The Minister will no doubt wish to discuss the matter with me and I would look foolish indeed if he knew more about it than I.'

Gautier tried to remember what he had put in the report. As far as he could recall there were only two things which he had not mentioned to Courtrand that morning, the cigarette case Surat had found and the half-finished letter which had been lying on the desk in Lady Dorothy's suite. He told Courtrand about the letter.

'What did the letter say?' Courtrand asked and when Gautier had given him the gist of what Lady Dorothy had written he continued: 'Do you know this Hotel de Lascombes?'

'No, Monsieur le Directeur, but I have made enquiries about it this afternoon. It is a place of low repute, a male brothel.'

'Gautier, you cannot be serious!'

'Yes, there is no doubt about that. And these initials J-J. T. refer to a Monsieur Jean-Jacques Touraine, a homosexual poet and author.'

Flinching, Courtrand screwed his face up in disgust. Then he said decisively, 'This letter cannot in any way be connected with Lady Dorothy's murder.'

'You do not think so?'

'It is unbelievable that a woman of excellent family could in any way be involved in such matters. There must be some other explanation. Either you have misunderstood what she wrote or the letter was not even written by her.'

Courtrand's belief in the incorruptibility of the upper echelons of society was unshakeable and if he was confronted with evidence that suggested he was wrong, he did not attempt to sweep it under the carpet, he simply ignored it. Gautier knew better than to argue with him, but he was sufficiently irritated not to wish to discuss the matter any further. He decided there was no point in even mentioning the cigarette case to Courtrand.

'I am convinced that her companion murdered Lady Dorothy,' Courtrand said. 'The simplest explanation is always the most likely in these cases. Have you questioned the woman again?'

'Not yet, Monsieur, but I have sent for her and she may even now be waiting in my office.'

'Then start questioning her at once. I would see her myself but I have been invited to dinner this evening and must leave the office early. If she confesses, and I daresay she will, arrest her immediately. And I will expect a full report on my desk tomorrow morning.'

As he went upstairs to his own office, Gautier decided that if Courtrand had to leave the Sûreté in the middle of the afternoon to prepare for it, then his invitation to dinner must be from a very important person, a minister of the government perhaps or a banker or a diplomat. On such occasions the director-general's barber was summoned to his home to trim and singe his beard and to wax his moustaches. In spite of his paunchy middle-age, Courtrand continued to behave like a dandy, having his beard trimmed and his nails manicured frequently and sending his evening dress shirts to London so that they could be laundered by an establishment which, he had been told, provided the same service for Buckingham Palace.

When he reached his office, Gautier found Miss Newbolt waiting for him. She was wearing a hat, as any lady would who went out during the day, but the hat she had chosen, a black straw with a curled-up brim and a large feather set at a jaunty angle, did not seem entirely suitable in the circumstances of her visit to the Sûreté. Gautier wondered whether the choice was deliberate, a small act of defiance.

'Did my assistant, Surat, not accompany you here, Mademoiselle?' he asked her.

'No, he remained behind at the hotel. I understand you instructed him to search my room.'

'I told him to ask you whether you had any objection to it being searched—and the room of Lady Dorothy's maid as well.'

'He did ask and of course I agreed.'

'I had intended that you should be there while he searched the room. It would have been better if you had.'

'Why should I? I have nothing to hide.'

'I never supposed that you had, Mademoiselle, but it is part of our usual police procedure.' She inclined her head and smiled and he realized that she did not believe him, so he changed the subject and asked her: 'Have you notified Lady Dorothy's family of her death?'

'I have. I telegraphed the Countess of Tain this morning and I have had a reply. A lawyer is being sent over to deal with the matter.'

'A lawyer? Is no member of the family coming to Paris?'

'They want things handled as quickly and as quietly as possible. Lady Dorothy's death could scarcely have come at a more inopportune time.'

'In what way?'

'There has been talk of a royal marriage for Lady Dorothy's niece; one of the young princes of Europe. Any unfortunate publicity or scandal will certainly delay the delicate family negotiations that have been taking place.'

'In that case it was most inconsiderate of Lady Dorothy to choose this time to be murdered.'

The gentle irony of Gautier's remark amused Miss Newbolt and she laughed. 'I do believe you're a radical, Monsieur Gautier. Do you disapprove of the aristocracy?'

'I do not, Mademoiselle, but I suspect that you do.'

'What makes you think that?'

'You made it clear when we spoke this morning that you hated Lady Dorothy.'

Miss Newbolt's face clouded over with discontent. For a time she said nothing but stared at her hands which lay in her lap, frowning as though she were brooding over past wrongs. When she frowned small wrinkles formed at the corners of her eyes and they seemed to accentuate the weariness in the eyes themselves and project her face into premature middle age. Gautier wondered how old she was; not much past thirty certainly, but suddenly she seemed nearer forty.

'That's different,' she said at last. 'A personal hatred. I hated her for what she was; a tyrant, mean, spiteful and without any of the graciousness one might have expected from a woman of her upbringing.'

'Then why did you work for her?'

Miss Newbolt raised her eyes and looked at him steadily. 'Monsieur Gautier, my father is a country clergyman with a large family—nine children. I am the eldest of four girls. All three of my younger sisters married and I was left single, so I had to find employment. I thought of becoming a school teacher but then through the good offices of my father's bishop, I was given the opportunity to go and work for Lady Dorothy. Can you blame me for accepting? I would live in a good home with plenty of servants and, or so I thought, opportunities to travel and meet interesting and important people.'

'But you were wrong?'

'I was right about the home and the travelling but Lady Dorothy had, as you French say, a thoroughly unpleasant character. She took pleasure in humiliating me, treated me like a servant, criticized my dress and my manners, poured scorn on my opinions.'

She began cataloguing all the slights and humiliations that Lady Dorothy had inflicted on her, giving examples and even citing dates and places. It was as though, with the death of her employer, the dam of self-restraint had collapsed releasing the flood of all the grievances that had accumulated over the years. And as Miss Newbolt talked, Gautier felt he could detect a change in her, as though a little of the self-assurance and independence which had been crushed by Lady Dorothy's petty tyranny was returning. A butterfly emerging from its chrysalis he thought, no not a butterfly but a soft, grey moth. The analogy amused him.

'More than anything,' Miss Newbolt concluded, 'Lady Dorothy despised me because I was unmarried. I had been left on the shelf, as we say in England.'

'But she was a spinster herself!'

'I know and she seemed to want to work out on me all the resentment she felt at not having been married herself.'

Gautier had deliberately been letting her talk without interruption. He was a patient man who was always ready to listen to people talking about themselves, for one could learn much about them, not so much from what they said as from what they did not care to say. Now he decided with some reluctance that it was time to take charge of the conversation and exercise a little pressure on the Englishwoman.

'You told me that you were soon to leave Lady Dorothy's employment.'

'That's right.'

'And that you were leaving at your own wish.'

'Yes. There is a limit to the humiliation which one can endure.'

'I have to tell you, Mademoiselle, that I found a half-finished letter which Lady Dorothy had been writing. In it she said she had dismissed you.'

For a moment it seemed as though Miss Newbolt were going to protest or argue. Then the tiny spurt of anger in her face subsided, she flushed and looked away. She accepted that accusation as she had no doubt accepted many rebukes, abjectly, like a dog that had been bullied into submission.

'Why did you lie?' Gautier's question, in spite of himself, was almost gentle.

'Pride, vanity, call it what you like,' Miss Newbolt's voice was bitter.

'What were her reasons for dismissing you?'

'I don't really know. One day she just flared up, lost her temper, told me I was incompetent and that I was to leave my situation as soon as we returned from Europe. No doubt she would have sent me packing on the spot had she been able to find anyone else to accompany her on her voyage.'

'So then you had another reason for hating her?'

Miss Newbolt looked at him and smiled bitterly. 'I've played into your hands, Inspector, have I not?'

'In what way?'

'I've told you I hated Lady Dorothy and I've lied to you. So now you will have decided that it was I who killed her. You found me by her body covered in blood and I have a motive for wishing her dead. That should be enough for you to arrest me.'

'I have decided nothing, Mademoiselle,' Gautier said.

He might have told her that in his experience revenge was not a common motive for murder and that when people killed for revenge more often than not they did so impulsively, while anger for the wrong which they felt had been done to them was still hot. And if Miss Newbolt had brooded over the way Lady Dorothy had treated her and decided on revenge, she would surely have planned a less clumsy murder. Gautier had already concluded that if Miss Newbolt had killed her employer, it must have been for some motive more compelling than revenge.

'What will happen now?' Miss Newbolt asked.

'The decision is not for me to make. A juge d'instruction is being appointed to examine the affair and after studying my report he will no doubt wish to question you himself.'

As Gautier was speaking they heard a knock on the door and Surat came into the room. When he saw Miss Newbolt he appeared embarrassed and looked first at her and then at Gautier in confusion.

'What is it, Surat?'

'We found this at the hotel, patron,' Surat replied.

He had been holding something which he had thrust hastily behind his back when he saw Miss Newbolt. Now he held it out and Gautier saw that it was a large brown envelope that had been sealed and then ripped open. There were stains on the envelope which might have been dried blood.

'That looks like the envelope in which Lady Dorothy brought back the money from the bank,' Miss Newbolt remarked.

'It contains several thousand francs in new notes,' Surat said.

'Where did you find it?'

'In this young lady's room. It had been pushed into the space between the back of the wardrobe and the wall.'

4

THE HOTEL DE LASCOMBES was in a little-known street not far from the Gare St. Lazare, but still within comfortable walking distance from the exclusive district around the Madeleine. Although the street led off Boulevard Haussmann, named in honour of the man whom Napoleon III had commissioned to pull down the centre of Paris and replace it with broad, majestic boulevards, it appeared somehow to have escaped Haussmann's attention and was narrow and ill-lit, a definite asset to a hotel most of whose visitors would prefer not to be seen entering or leaving it. Gautier knew it was a male brothel and also that unlike many other 'maisons de tolerance' which catered for both inverts and those of more normal inclinations, it had seldom, if ever, been troubled by the police. This led him to suppose that the place must be under the 'protection' of someone important.

The hotel took in the top three storeys of a building with shops below it and was reached by a flight of stairs which led into a small vestibule. When Gautier arrived the owner of the hotel was seated behind the reception desk. André Moncade was a Breton who had come to Paris as a young man to go into service. He had become one of a squad of eight beautiful footmen working for one of society's most notorious inverts, the Duc de Narbonne. The duc was popularly known as The Ambassador of Sodom and it was said that he gave each of his footmen a pearl necklace every year. On his own admission blackmail cost him 70,000 francs a year. When he was in his thirties and losing his hair and his good looks, Moncade had used the money he had extracted from the duc to buy a modest hotel and turn it into a male brothel. There he would arrange rendezvous for gentlemen from society with obliging young chauffeurs and hairdressers and postmen.

When Gautier had introduced himself Moncade said: 'We had

better go to my study, Inspector, where we will not be disturbed.'

He shouted and a young man appeared through a door at the back of the vestibule and took his place behind the reception desk. Moncade's office was on the second storey of the hotel and it was not so much an office as a private drawing-room, decorated with taste and furnished for comfort. Among the paintings which hung on the walls Gautier recognized a Matisse and a Renoir, two artists whose work had become fashionable and now commanded high prices. When Moncade offered him a glass of port, Gautier accepted. If a man wished to be friendly there was no point in discouraging him.

'What do you know of Lady Dorothy Strathy?' he asked him.

'Strathy? The name means nothing to me.'

'She has been in Paris and has been making enquiries about your hotel.'

'What possible interest could she have in my modest establishment?' Moncade grinned slyly. 'As you know, Inspector, we do not cater for the tastes of ladies here.'

'I was hoping you might be able to answer that.'

'I can only hazard a guess. What if the lady had heard that her husband was in the habit of using my hotel when he was in Paris? We have a number of English gentlemen among our clients. Might she be trying to get proof of his behaviour? She could be contemplating divorce.'

'The lady in question is not married.'

'Very strange!'

'But she did have a brother. The Earl of Tain. He died not long ago.'

'Once again, Inspector, I do not know the name. But, as you will understand, the gentlemen who visit my establishment seldom use their proper names and I make it a rule that we never refer even to the names which they give us as their own. My staff have nicknames for most of our clients.'

'Nicknames?'

'Yes. For example, one client who is particularly lavish with his tips is known to us as "God's Gift". Then there are two German gentlemen who always arrive together. "The Lorelie" is the name we've chosen for them.'

Moncade's answers were prompt and confident. The confidence could have been that of a man who knew he was telling the truth or of one well practised in lying. Gautier was going to reserve his judgement on the man's honesty until he had more reliable evidence. He could not help feeling, though, that a man as shrewd as Moncade would make it his business to find out the name and background of any prominent person who used his hotel regularly, if only as a precaution against being left with unpaid bills or having his hotel dragged into any scandal so sensational that the police could not ignore it.

'You can think of no other possible reason for the lady's interest in the Hotel de Lascombes then?' he asked him.

'Only one. Did you say that her brother, this earl, is dead?'

'Yes, he died some months ago I understand.'

Moncade nodded thoughtfully. 'For some years now, Inspector, a letter has been arriving every month without fail from London, always at the beginning of the month. I told myself that perhaps these letters contained a payment in some form, possibly from a bank, because they came in what looked like business envelopes with a typewritten address. Then not long ago, a few months I suppose, there was no letter at the beginning of the month. Since then there have been no more.'

'And you believe they could have been sent here on the instructions of the Earl of Tain?'

'It is possible. Why not? That would explain why the letters suddenly stopped arriving. The earl is dead.'

The explanation was plausible, too plausible and too pat for Moncade to have just thought of it. Gautier sensed that he was being told the truth. He asked the hotelier: 'To whom were the letters addressed?'

'A Monsieur Decartier.'

'And did this Decartier call at your hotel to collect them?'

'No. In fact I have never met the gentleman. I agreed to allow him to use the hotel as an address because a friend of his, one of my clients, asked me to. Decartier sent someone to pick up the letters for him. At one time he merely gave some street urchin a few sous to collect them and take them to him. More recently it had been a housemaid. One supposes that Decartier, whoever he is, had moved up in the world, helped no doubt by the money he had been extorting.'

'Are you suggesting it was blackmail?'

'It seems likely.' Moncade shrugged his shoulders and spread his hands expressively. 'In the kind of relationships which flourish in a hotel like mine, there is always the ultimate possibility of blackmail.'

'Blackmailers are not usually content to take their money in small sums over a long period. They grow greedy and bleed their victims quickly for as much as they can afford.'

'Are you making these enquiries on behalf of this English milady?' Moncade asked and Gautier wondered why he had not put the question to him before.

'No, she is dead. She was stabbed to death in her hotel early this morning.'

'You did not tell me that,' Moncade said reproachfully.

Either he was genuinely disconcerted by the news of Lady Dorothy's murder or he was a skilled dissembler. Gautier's instincts told him that although the man had been speaking the truth it had not been the whole truth. He tried to think of a way of flushing it out.

'You know the poet Jean-Jacques Touraine, I believe.'

'Yes,' Moncade agreed cautiously.

'I was speaking to him this afternoon. It would appear that he knows of your hotel.'

'He used to visit us regularly, but that was some years ago.'

'Did you not say that you preferred not to know the names of your clients?'

'Monsieur Touraine was different. He did not use the hotel in the same way as other clients do. You might say he was more of a friend.' Having chosen the answer he would make to Gautier's question, Moncade then began to elaborate on it, as though a wealth of circumstantial detail would reinforce its credibility. 'More than once I was able to do the gentleman a service when he was in difficulties and he was grateful. To repay me he often recommended my hotel to people whom he met.'

With difficulty, Gautier repressed a sigh. He knew that Moncade was going to tell him the story of how he had helped

Touraine and guessed that even if the story were true, it would have no possible bearing on Lady Dorothy's murder. He was right. Moncade told him how one evening some years previously, Touraine had met two young men in a café and been tricked into going with them to a cellar in a shady street not far from Gare St. Lazare. The young men were not, as Touraine supposed, homosexuals and once in the cellar they had forced him to hand over to them all the money he was carrying and then stripped him of his clothes and taken them as well. Left naked in the cellar, Touraine had attracted the attention of a small boy in the street and sent him to the Hotel de Lascombes for help.

'I went to the cellar myself,' Moncade said, 'and found him there wrapped only in a sheet of dirty newspaper. It was the funniest spectacle you could imagine! We rescued him and later I was able to trace the young men who had robbed him and he had his clothes returned.'

'How long is it since you have seen Touraine?'

'Why do you ask?'

'He was commissioned by Lady Dorothy to make certain enquiries about her late brother.'

Moncade hesitated, but only momentarily. One sensed that he was trying to decide whether to improvise another evasion to Gautier's question or to lie or to tell the truth. Then he made up his mind and smiled.

'That explains something which has been puzzling me, Inspector.'

'What was that?'

'Monsieur Touraine came here last evening and asked me several questions about an Englishman who might have visited the hotel. He did not mention any name though.'

'What did you tell him?'

'What could I tell him, Inspector? As I have already explained to you, I know nothing.'

That evening Gautier dined with Madame Michelle Le Tellier in her apartment in Rue Miromesnil. Madame Le Tellier was a widow whose husband, a newspaper editor, had been shot and killed by a young woman. His murder had been one in a series of incidents devised by a small group of conspirators as part of a plot to bring down the government and usurp power themselves, a plot which had been discovered and frustrated by Gautier. In the course of his investigations he had met and become friendly with Madame Le Tellier and now he dined regularly at her home, tête-à-tête and discreetly, for she was still supposed to be in mourning for her late husband.

Although she was an intelligent woman and in many ways a liberal thinker, Madame Le Tellier felt obliged to pay lip service at least to the conventions of Paris society which dictated that for months after her husband's death a widow should always wear black, leave her house only when chaperoned and never accept invitations nor entertain guests. By inviting a man to dine with her alone, she was breaking all the rules and usually she compounded her offence by wearing brightly coloured evening gowns and the best of her jewellery.

'Did Suzanne want children?' she asked Gautier.

'Very much, I think.'

'Do you suppose it would have made any difference to your marriage if there had been children?'

'Probably, yes.'

Rather more than two years previously Gautier's wife, Suzanne, had left him and gone to live with a former policeman named Gaston. Now she and her lover owned a small café in an unprepossessing part of Pigalle and from time to time Gautier would visit them, not because he enjoyed doing so but because it gave Suzanne pleasure to think that they could all three remain friends.

Sometimes when they dined together and during the lovemaking which often followed, Michelle Le Tellier would ask Gautier about his wife and about their marriage and he was beginning to believe that it was through more than just curiosity. He knew that she wondered why he had never divorced Suzanne. Probably she did not realize that divorces were difficult to arrange and costly, a luxury for the affluent and well connected, and that if he were to start divorce proceedings they could easily mean that Suzanne would be brought into court on charges of adultery. He had no wish to humiliate her, especially now that she was expecting a child. Suzanne had been pregnant for some months and for a reason which he could not explain he had never mentioned the fact to Michelle Le Tellier.

When they had almost finished dinner she remarked: 'Something rather odd happened earlier this evening. The Comte de Bouttin called on me.'

'But you are not supposed to receive visitors as long as you are in mourning, not gentlemen visitors certainly.'

'Of course not. I didn't receive him, but he left his card.'

'Do you know why he called?'

'I have no idea. I scarcely know the man. But—and this makes it all the more odd—he asked my maid who opened the door to him a whole string of questions.'

'About what?'

'Everything. Whether I received any visitors, who they were, what time of day they called, whether I ever went out and if so how often and with whom.'

Gautier laughed. 'Perhaps he is planning for the day when you come out of mourning.'

'What do you mean?'

'He may be looking for a second wife to support him.'

'Me!' Michelle exclaimed incredulously. 'What little money I have would never run to his expensive tastes.'

Comte Sébastien de Bouttin was well-known in Paris society. Handsome, proud but impoverished, he was almost all that remained of one of the great noble families of France which had managed to survive the Revolution. Some years previously he had married the only daughter of an American railroad millionaire and had lived in style on her fortune, building an ostentatiously luxurious house on the edge of the Bois de Boulogne, buying yachts, racehorses, paintings, automobiles whenever the mood took him. In less than five years he had gone through 60 million francs until finally his wife, encouraged by her relatives and tired of his endless petty infidelities, had thrown him out of their home, divorced him and married a Russian prince.

'Evidently I must keep an eye on this scoundrel,' Gautier said jokingly. 'He may have designs on you.'

'Would you mind if he had?'

'Certainly. I can be as jealous as the next man.'

She shook her head. 'Not you, Jean-Paul. You're too detached, too self-sufficient.'

'Have I not given you proof enough of my passion?'

'Of your passion, yes. But you are not possessive. Success with women has been too easy for you. If one slips from your grasp, there is always another close at hand.'

'You make them sound like umbrellas,' Gautier grumbled.

Although her tone was mocking, Gautier thought he detected beneath her banter a hint of discontent and he wondered what had provoked the mood. Whatever it was, she appeared to shrug it off and they began to talk of other things, of books and the theatre and of the rumours that a ballet company from Russia would be coming to perform in Paris. After dinner they moved to the drawing-room and she smoked a cigarette while Gautier drank a glass of cognac.

She was sitting on a chaise-longue and when after a time he went and sat on the edge of it, she allowed him to take the combs out of her hair so that it fell to her shoulders and to unbutton her corsage as he had on other evenings. Her breasts were large. She often complained of what she described as her Teutonic beauty; blue eyes, pink complexion, fair hair and full-breasted figure; a Wagner heroine. The scent of her sharpened Gautier's desire.

'Who was it,' he whispered, 'who spoke of the comfort of the double-bed comparing it with the rough and tumble of the chaise-longue?'

She smiled briefly and then looked at him, her expression serious. 'Not tonight, Jean-Paul. Do you mind?'

'Of course not.' He smiled and sighed to show his disappointment.

'Thank you.' She kissed him lightly on the cheek. 'I'm sure you can find another umbrella not too far away.'

Once again he sensed that behind the gesture and the words lay a feeling which she was keeping in check but which she did not wish wholly to disguise; displeasure or irritation at something he had done or failed to do. He left her soon afterwards and she let him out of the apartment herself, for she had allowed the servants to go to bed.

When he bent over to kiss her hand she said: 'There, you see! You didn't really wish to make love tonight at all.'

'How can you say that?'

'If you had wished to, you would not have accepted my refusal so calmly.'

As, after leaving her apartment, Gautier walked past the Elysée Palace towards Place de la Concorde, he found himself wondering whether he had upset Michelle in any way. She was an intelligent woman, generous and understanding and not given to petulance. Perhaps she believed that he had failed her, although he had no idea how. After all, he supposed that he must have failed Suzanne as well or she would never have left him.

Deciding that he would walk home to his apartment along the Left Bank, he crossed the Seine by the Pont de la Concorde and paused half way to look down over the parapet of the bridge towards the river. There was no moon that night and he could scarcely see the water, only the dull gleam on its surface as it moved slowly, menacingly it seemed, through the dark city. Outwardly, Paris was sleeping but he knew that greed and lust and viciousness never slumbered and even at that moment in some dark alley the apache's knife was striking or behind shuttered windows drunken hands were tightening around a woman's throat.

Shaking off his gloom, he crossed to the Left Bank and walked through deserted streets to his apartment. As he climbed the stairs of the building, he felt that familiar depression which always assailed him when he returned alone to an empty home. In the years since Suzanne had left him, he had not always been alone. There had been other women, never casual encounters but women who, for a time, usually a brief time, had been his mistress; Claudine, an artists' model from Montmartre; Juliette Prévot, a novelist; Janine, whose mother had owned a café in Place Dauphine.

When he reached the apartment and saw a light shining under the door he was surprised. Only one of his neighbours, a woman who came to tidy the place and who sometimes shopped for him, had a key to the apartment and he had never known her to be so careless as to leave one of the gas lamps burning. He was even more surprised when he opened the door and saw that he had a visitor, his father-in-law. He had always been fond of Monsieur Duclos and regretted very much that after his marriage failed he had lost touch with the old man.

'Your neighbour allowed me to wait here,' Monsieur Duclos said apologetically as they shook hands.

'You've brought me news of Suzanne,' Gautier guessed and he saw at once from the anguish on the old man's face that the news was not good. 'Don't tell me she lost the child!'

'No. The baby was born prematurely and it's a boy. But Suzanne is dead.'

5

IN HIS OFFICE next morning Gautier forced himself to concentrate on his work. The reports he had to write and to read seemed meaningless, an exercise in futility and for the first time that he could recall since joining the Sûreté he felt a revulsion against what he was being asked to do. The murder of an Englishwoman, an aristocrat, was of little consequence; her going had left the world no poorer and finding her murderer would do no more than satisfy justice. It would do nothing to comfort or relieve the misery of thousands of ordinary people who even then were crushed by their own griefs.

He recognized his mood for what it was, a depression caused not so much by sorrow as by guilt and remorse. Suzanne's father had kept him up until four that morning, talking of his daughter with a lack of emotion that was painful to watch. Gautier had kept wishing that the man would break down and cry. Instead, Monsieur Duclos had talked on, recounting stories of Suzanne's childhood, of the love she had always shown for her parents, of her little naughtinesses, of the hopes they had held for her.

Not until he had finally risen to leave and taken Gautier's hand in his own two, had his voice choked a little. 'In all her life she only made me unhappy once. That was when she left you, Jean-Paul, for Gaston.'

The remark was sincere and, no doubt, meant to console, but it only added to Gautier's depression and his sense of guilt. He could not help thinking that if he had been a better husband to Suzanne, had not left her alone so much, had not indulged in the occasional infidelities which she did not know about but may have guessed, she would not have left him and would still be alive. The flaw in that line of reasoning was that she might have left him anyway because he had not given her the child she wanted, but he shut his mind to the idea. The knowledge that the previous night, while she had been dying, he had been dining with another woman and would, had she allowed it, have slept with her, only added to his remorse.

When he had arrived in his office earlier that morning, he had read the report which Surat had left for him on the enquiries he had made among the staff of the Hotel Cheltenham. What he had learned did not amount to much. One chambermaid admitted to passing a man in waiter's uniform, whom she had never seen in the hotel before and did not know, on the servants' stairs between the entresol and the first floor. He had been carrying a breakfast tray. Another maid was less certain but thought she had also seen a strange waiter on the fifth floor but without a breakfast tray. The descriptions which both girls had given of the unknown waiter were not dissimilar: medium height, heavily built and with a complexion dark enough to suggest at least a touch of Algerian blood.

Gautier had spoken with Surat, gone though the report with him and then sent him off to make enquiries among the staff of the Hotel de Lascombes and any clients who might be around, to find out if anything were known of the Monsieur Decartier who had been receiving money from London. It was a slender hope. People who were in any way connected with a notorious male brothel would be reluctant even to talk to the police. Moreover, Gautier was far from certain that there was a Monsieur Decartier. Part of what Moncade had told him was certainly untrue, the improvisation of a skilful liar, but if there was any substance in Moncade's story, Surat, with his capacity for making friends with people from all stations in life and his quiet persistence, was the man most likely to separate the truth from the fiction.

Not long after Surat had left, Gautier had had a second interview with Jean-Jacques Touraine, which was as unsatisfactory as the first one had been. The poet had arrived at the Sûreté in combative mood, fortified perhaps by the arrival of his mother in Paris, but Gautier had soon been able to shatter his bravado.

'From enquiries we have made, Monsieur,' he had told him, 'I know you lied to me when we discussed this affair yesterday.'

Touraine had feigned indignation. 'How can you say that?'

'You told me you did not know what enquiries Lady Dorothy

wished you to make, yet you had already been to the Hotel de Lascombes asking questions on her behalf.'

'Who told you that?'

'I visited the hotel myself after speaking with you.'

'As I told you, the English milady asked me to treat our conversation as confidential,' Touraine had replied sullenly.

'That need not concern you now that she is dead.'

'I am not obliged to tell you anything.'

'As you please. You may tell me now or return to answer the questions of the juge d'instruction this afternoon.'

Eventually, in the face of Gautier's threat, and worried perhaps that his mother might get to hear of it if he paid a second visit to the Sûreté in one day, Touraine had reluctantly given way. What he had to say had not added much to what Gautier already knew but it did at least confirm some of what Moncade had told him. When the Earl of Tain had died, his widow the countess had discovered that his bank, on the earl's instructions, had been making a payment each month to a Monsieur Decartier care of the Hotel de Lascombes.

The sums paid out each month had not been large, according to Lady Dorothy, but even so they were more than the earl, whose family through the years had gradually become impoverished largely because of the extravagant and profligate way of life of the male members, could afford. The countess, fearing a scandal would endanger her daughter's marriage prospects, had decided she must find out as discreetly as possible to whom the money was being sent and why. She and Lady Dorothy had assumed that the money was being paid in response to blackmail and had concluded, for reasons of their own, that the blackmailer must be exploiting some homosexual indiscretions which the earl had committed while on a visit to Paris.

Touraine, like Moncade, had maintained that he did not know the identity of the mysterious Monsieur Decartier. Gautier had been certain that at least one of them, if not both, was lying, but he had decided to let the matter rest for the present and to hope that Surat might trace the man. Later, if it proved necessary, he might be able to put more pressure on Touraine by bringing him before a juge d'instruction.

Now, after finishing yet another report on the progress of the investigations, he took it down to the director-general's office. There he learnt from Corbin that Courtrand had been sent for by the Minister of Justice. The English lawyer representing Lady Dorothy's family, Corbin said, had arrived in Paris that morning and after speaking to Miss Newbolt, had arranged through the personal intervention of the British Ambassador, a meeting with the minister.

'You may also like to know,' Corbin said, 'that Judge Dussart has been appointed juge d'instruction in the matter of the English-woman's death.'

'Dussart? A pity!'

'Why do you say that?'

'I had hoped it might be Judge Loubet. He's easy to work with and I like him.'

'Well, it's Dussart. It seems he asked for the assignment. You are to report to him in his rooms at the Ministry this afternoon.'

As he left the room, Gautier felt even more depressed. Decisions were now being taken at a higher level about the murder of Lady Dorothy. He would still be working on the case but under the direction of the juge d'instruction and he had always preferred having a free hand to conduct enquiries in his own way. Surrendering to gloom, he decided there was nothing useful he could do until he saw Judge Dussart that afternoon and, since it was almost midday, he left the Sûreté for the Café Corneille.

As he crossed the Seine to the Left Bank, he recalled that it was there, all those months ago, that Suzanne's father had told him that she wished to leave him. She had sent the old man to break the news because she could not bear to do it herself. Suzanne had been too soft-hearted to enjoy adultery and too well brought up not to have a sense of shame. Now she had proved that she had not been strong enough physically to have children. Gautier's sense of guilt returned as he told himself that if he had been loving enough and attentive enough to have kept her affection she would still be alive.

When he reached the Café Corneille, it was still too early for most of the regular habitués to be there and he found Duthrey alone at their usual table. When they shook hands the journalist held his for a moment and looked at him.

'Old friend,' he said. 'I have heard the news about your wife. I am desolate.'

'You are very kind. Thank you.'

Gautier did not ask how Duthrey had heard about Suzanne's death and they made no further mention of the matter. Although most of his friends who went to the café must have known that his wife had left him, none of them would have felt that they knew him intimately enough to have expressed their sympathy at her death. And yet, Gautier thought, the French were supposed to be a demonstrative race.

He and Duthrey began to talk of the position of the Catholic Church in France. Duthrey had a special interest in religion and he was writing a series of articles for *Figaro* on the changes in the relationship between church and state since the fall of the Third Empire. Gautier was no historian, nor theologian either, but his views were of interest to Duthrey, who wished to present the situation as it was seen by ordinary people.

While they were talking, two men came into the café and sat down at the table next to their own. The face of one of the men was familiar, although Gautier could not put a name to it. He was slim and good looking, in his late thirties in all probability, with fair hair and a small fair moustache, the ends of which had been waxed into two points as fine and as sharp as knitting-needles. He carried a black cane with a silver knob and wore a monocle which he took out of his eye and waved whenever he wished to emphasize whatever he was saying and which exaggerated the arrogance of his expression. The other man was older, fatter and uglier and seemed to be following his companion about as an ageing bulldog follows its master.

Presently Froissart, the bookseller, arrived to join Gautier and Duthrey. The conversation shifted from religion to poetry and they discussed a recently published volume of verse by Lucie Delarue-Mardrus which was receiving generous praise from reviewers.

Suddenly, without warning, the fair-haired man reached out and tapped Gautier on the shoulder with his cane. 'Are you Gautier?' he demanded.

As Gautier looked round in surprise, he recognized the face. It was the Comte de Bouttin. He remembered Michelle Le Tellier saying the previous evening that the comte had been round at her house asking questions about her friends.

'Yes, Monsieur. I'm Gautier.'

'Then tell me, is it true that the Sûreté is providing a new kind of service these days?' the comte asked insolently.

'What kind of service?'

'Keeping the beds of lovely widows warm while they are in mourning.'

Gautier turned away. Either the comte was drunk, which did not seem likely at that time of day, or he wished to provoke a scene. In either case it would be wise to ignore him. But the gesture did not succeed in deflecting the comte from whatever he intended. Instead, having a police inspector turn his back on him seemed to drive him into a fury. He struck Gautier across the forearm with his cane, more forcibly this time.

'I'm speaking to you, do you hear?'

Gautier felt the slow surge of anger rising. On any other day and with almost anyone else but the comte provoking him, he would have controlled it. He turned and faced the comte again.

'Kindly keep your remarks to yourself, Monsieur,' he said coldly. 'My friends and I do not find them amusing.'

'They say you are obliging Madame Le Tellier. Are there other ladies who invite you to their beds as well?'

The mention of Michelle Le Tellier's name, a deliberate breach of etiquette and a calculated insult to the lady, was too much for Gautier's self-restraint. He said angrily: 'At least no lady has ever had to pay for any service I may have rendered her, Monsieur.'

'Oh yes?'

'On the other hand, 60 million francs was the fee your wife had to pay, I understand.'

The comte leapt to his feet, brandishing his cane. There could be no doubting that his fury was genuine now. For a moment it seemed as though he would strike Gautier with the cane, but some instinct, a legacy of his upbringing, saved him from disgracing himself. Instead he checked his arm, pulled out a visiting card which he seemed to have ready in a waistcoat pocket and flung it on the table in front of Gautier.

'My seconds will call on you, Monsieur,' he said and then,

turning away, he walked out of the café followed by his shambling companion.

The comte's raised voice and the dramatic challenge to a duel had startled everyone in the café. There were cafés in Paris which were frequented by flamboyant characters, actors, circus performers, automobile racing drivers, but the Café Corneille was not one of them. Most of its habitués were men of intellect rather than action, not given to displays of bravado. Everyone, the customers, the waiters, the wife of the proprietor seated at the desk where she collected the money and did accounts, was silent and they were all looking at Gautier. Slowly he picked up the comte's card and stared at it, aware that it was a meaningless gesture and feeling stupidly self-conscious.

'My friend,' he said to Duthrey, trying not to make what he was going to say seem like a public pronouncement, 'would you do me the honour of acting as one of my seconds?'

6

THAT AFTERNOON BECAME for Gautier a confused series of fragmentary incidents, seemingly unrelated, which followed each other in unpatterned sequence. For much of the time he was only dimly aware of what was happening and he went about his duties mechanically. Knowing that he had committed himself to fighting a duel produced no sensation of physical fear, for the situation seemed totally unreal. It was as though he were moving in a dream world peopled by shadowy figures whose words and actions were to be watched but not taken seriously.

At the Café Corneille that morning, after the Comte de Bouttin had left, Duthrey and Froissart had tried to persuade him not to go through with the duel. Duelling was against the law and even though the authorities usually chose to ignore the many dawn confrontations that took place in the Bois de Boulogne or behind the grandstand at one of the racecourses, they could not be expected to condone a police officer taking part in one. If his duel with the comte became known, Gautier, even if he escaped injury, could expect at the very least a severe reprimand and possibly demotion in rank or even dismissal.

He had not listened to his friends' arguments and knew that they thought he was being perverse and unreasonable. How could he have explained his reasons to them: that the guilt he felt for having failed one woman would be expiated by defending another? Gautier had never had a very high regard for the conventions of society. The vanity of men in protecting what they saw as their honour but which in reality was no more than a ridiculous pride, had always amused him. Now he was aping their behaviour without any sense of shame. The irony of the fact that it was his wife whom he had failed and his mistress whose honour and good name he would be defending had not escaped him but neither had it shaken his resolve.

'I cannot go on living for ever in the protection of my position as a police officer,' he had told Duthrey and Froissart.

While they had been arguing, two men had arrived in the café to speak with him. They had presented their cards and told Gautier that they would be acting as the Comte de Bouttin's seconds in this affair of honour. The comte, they had explained, was leaving for America very soon and wished to have the duel fought before he left. Would the next morning suit Monsieur Gautier, they asked, at six in the Bois de Boulogne? Duthrey, speaking on behalf of Gautier, had accepted but reluctantly. The comte's seconds had then pointed out that Gautier had the choice of weapons.

'We will need time to discuss that,' Duthrey had replied. 'I will inform you of Monsieur Gautier's choice before the afternoon is over.'

From the Café Corneille Gautier, missing out lunch, had returned to the Sûreté where, as an aid to his memory, he made notes on every step so far taken in the investigation of Lady Dorothy's murder and the results they had produced. Then at two-thirty he went to Judge Dussart's rooms in the Ministry of Justice. He had only once before had Dussart as juge d'instruction in the case he had been investigating and had found the man pedantic and difficult. The judge had the cold, sour manner shared by spinsters and old men who had not lived up to their ambitions.

Dussart had been given copies of the reports Gautier had written on Lady Dorothy's murder, with the exception of the first one which Corbin had sent to the Minister of Justice and which, for some reason, could not now be found. He had read the reports, slowly and painstakingly, while Gautier had sat waiting and then gone over them, asking questions, many of them on trivial points which could not possibly help to establish the identity or the motives of the murderer. Scientific experts had examined the knife used to stab Lady Dorothy, which was an ordinary kitchen knife of a type that could be bought in scores of shops anywhere in Paris and Dussart had demanded why their report did not give the exact dimensions of the knife. He had also asked for a list showing the numbers and denominations of the bank notes found in Miss Newbolt's room. Then he had irritated Gautier by wanting to know what type of pen had been used by Lady Dorothy to write her unfinished letter and insisted that it should be produced for him to examine. Gautier had been glad that the cigarette case had not been mentioned in any of the reports Dussart saw, for that no doubt would have triggered off another volley of questions.

Finally, when his curiosity was satisfied and Gautier's patience almost at an end, Dussart had said, 'I will examine the woman Newbolt at ten o'clock tomorrow morning. See that she is brought here at that time.'

'And who will you wish to see after her, Monsieur?'

'That will depend on what conclusions I form. Probably no one except perhaps the English maid and in that case we will need an interpreter. From the evidence I have so far seen, it would appear that it was Newbolt who killed her mistress.'

'Do you wish that the English lawyer is present at her examination?'

'No. I have already spoken to him. He has not been sent here to help Newbolt. Lady Dorothy's family only want the matter to be concluded as discreetly and as quickly as possible.'

As he walked back to his office in the Sûreté, Gautier began to wonder about Dussart's attitude to the murder of Lady Dorothy. The normal procedure would be for the juge d'instruction to examine not only every suspect in a criminal case, but also all possible witnesses and anyone else whose testimony could have any bearing on the matter. This could take several days, even weeks in a complex case, following which a complete dossier would be sent to the Chambre des Mises en Accusations, where a decision would be taken on whether the evidence justified any suspect being indicted for the crime. Dussart's attitude, however, suggested that he had already tried Miss Newbolt and found her guilty. At any other time Gautier would be curious to know why, but that afternoon his natural inquisitiveness was stifled by persisting guilt and a strange sense of fatalism. By next morning when Dussart began to examine Miss Newbolt, he might already be dead. The thought did not disturb him.

Back at the Sûreté he found Duthrey waiting for him, together with Marigny, another journalist from *Figaro*. Marigny was a younger man, with a sharp wit and an excitable nature who had fought several duels himself and who had agreed to act as Gautier's other second. The two of them had come to take Gautier to the Club des Mousquetaires where Duthrey had arranged an appointment with the director, Maître Lavalier. The reputation of the Club des Mousquetaires was not very high among the upper strata of Paris society since its members, besides a number of actors and a few ambitious journalists, were mainly profligate younger sons of aristocratic families, but Maître Lavalier was recognized to be France's leading authority on the protocol of duelling.

When they arrived at the club and Duthrey had described the circumstances in which the challenge to a duel had been made, Lavalier said to Gautier, 'One gets the impression, Monsieur, that you were deliberately engineered into this affair.'

'Without a doubt.'

'That is quite wrong. Duels are intended as a means of settling differences between gentlemen, not for paying off old scores or appeasing jealousy. The Comte de Bouttin should know better.'

'Then would my friend be justified in refusing to fight?' Duthrey asked quickly.

'Not now the challenge has been accepted. It has become a matter of honour.'

'What happens next?'

Solemnly, in the manner of a high priest instructing an acolyte in the mysteries of the faith, Lavalier described every stage in a duel from the flinging down of the challenge to the breakfast of reconciliation when honour had been satisfied. He explained the behaviour that was expected of gentlemen, the finesse and the nuances which must be observed if the affair was to be conducted with decorum and dignity.

When it was over he asked Duthrey, 'What weapons are to be used?'

'As yet we have not decided.'

'Has your friend any skill with the sword?'

'Not as far as I know.'

'Then perhaps you should go downstairs to the Salle des Armes and take advice from Monsieur Jap.'

The Salle des Armes was in what had once been the cellars of the building; a narrow room with a low ceiling, lit by gas jets. Ranged around the room in racks mounted on the walls were épées and sabres, and a piste on which fencers could practise had been marked on the floor.

Monsieur Jap, the Maître d'Armes, was a small, wiry man, bald but with flourishing moustaches and he was dressed like a gymnast. Under his direction, Gautier took off his coat, waistcoat and cravat, strapped a protective padded plastron on his chest and put on one of the wire-mesh masks that fencers used in practice fights. Jap demonstrated how the épée should be held and made him stand with his right foot forward, knees slightly bent in what he described as a good 'on guard' position.

'First we will try the lunge, Monsieur,' he said, 'and then the parry.'

He made Gautier practise a few simple drills first and then he put on a mask and plastron and picked up an épée himself. 'Now Monsieur, you may try out what I have taught you on an opponent.'

It did not take long for both of them to realize the futility of what Jap was trying to do. Gautier's lunges were awkward, his parries wild and cumbersome. Jap could hit him at will and in a real duel an opponent with any measure of swordsmanship would have wounded him, perhaps mortally, within a few seconds.

'Monsieur,' Jap said at last, but courteously, 'my advice to you is to choose pistols for your engagement.'

'I have no experience of pistols either.'

'Even so, your chances of surviving would be greater. Sometimes quite expert shots are known to miss.'

'Jean-Paul, you must not go through with this charade,' Michelle Le Tellier pleaded.

'It is too late to withdraw now.'

When Gautier had arrived back at the Sûreté from the Club des Mousquetaires, he had found waiting for him a 'petit bleu', a message sent through the city's pneumatic telegraph system, from Madame Le Tellier. In it she asked him to go and see her that evening without fail. He had put off visiting her as long as he possibly could, sensing what she wished to say to him, and had only gone to Rue Miromesnil at ten o'clock so that any argument they might have would not be prolonged.

'For grown men to fight duels today is absurd!' Michelle protested.

'I agree with you.'

'Pistols at dawn in the woods, the ceremonial, the whole idea that honour can be satisfied by a flesh wound in the arm—it's infantile! An extension of schoolboy dreams!'

'Of course. What you say is true.'

'Then why did you allow yourself to be drawn into this madness?'

'The reasons are too difficult to explain.'

'Why not try? You owe me that at least.'

She was entitled to expect an explanation. Gautier knew that. He had accepted her friendship, taken her hospitality, slept with her and so she had a right to know why she had suddenly been made, through no choice of her own, a symbolic landmark in his life, a turning point, a *casus belli*. He did his best to tell her, starting with empty clichés about honour and pride, but refusing to shelter behind the pretence that he had chosen to fight a duel for her sake. Michelle listened patiently but unmoved. Finally, although he had to force himself to do so, he told her about Suzanne's death.

Instantly her expression changed. Scepticism softened into sympathy. They were standing in the drawing-room, facing each other, stiffly, like contestants. Now Michelle stepped forward and placed her hand on his shoulder.

'Chéri!' she exclaimed. 'I'm so sorry! Why didn't you tell me? Why didn't you come to me last night as soon as you heard?'

He knew then that although she cared for him, might well love him, she did not understand him. The grief, guilt and remorse which had haunted him ever since he had been told of Suzanne's death could never be exorcized in another woman's bed. And yet when she kissed him on the lips he knew that now he was going to take refuge in her sympathy, to allow himself to slip easily into the comforting warmth of whispered words and caresses which would, for a brief moment at least, shut out reality.

'You were right last night,' she said and she smiled as she took his hands and placed them on her breasts. 'The chaise-longue was never made for love!'

He let her lead him into the bedroom and there he undressed her, the gown first and then the undergarments, layers of them it seemed. He took them off slowly, as though it were a ritual, restraining his growing desire and caressing gently each part of her body as it was revealed. When finally she was naked, she pressed her body against his, her breathing fast and shallow. They lay on the bed and she wrapped her legs around him.

'I won't allow you to risk your life for me, Jean-Paul,' she whispered and the whisper was strangled in a gasp of pleasure.

He heard what she was saying but could not help comparing her eagerness with the way in which the previous night she had rejected him.

The noise of the horses' hooves striking the cobblestones rang through the deserted streets with a musical clarity, each note precisely pitched and in perfect rhythm. The dawn had been no more than a distant glimmer in a dark sky when Duthrey and Marigny had collected Gautier from his apartment in a closed carriage; not a fiacre because a fiacre, Duthrey had explained, would have provided neither the privacy needed for an illicit enterprise nor the dignity which the occasion demanded. Gautier was amused to observe how seriously Duthrey, a man who had always held violence in contempt, was taking his duties. He could see in his manner something of the same excitement, the fascination of death, that he had noticed in the staff of the Hotel Cheltenham on the morning when Lady Dorothy's body had been discovered.

After leaving Michelle Le Tellier, he had returned home for two or three hours of sleep before Duthrey had arrived. A night spent mainly in love, a love which had grown fiercer as Michelle's passion had seemed to heighten, fed by an excitement he had not known her show before, was not, he supposed, an ideal preparation for a duel. But he felt no fear, only the fatalism which had enveloped him ever since the Comte de Bouttin had thrown down his challenge.

As they drove down Avenue du Bois, the broad, tree-flanked avenue which led from Etoile to the Bois de Boulogne and in which some of the wealthiest men in France had built themselves imposing houses, the sky lightened. Dawn came with unusual swiftness, as though it were anxious not to miss the drama that was soon to be performed and by the time they reached the Bois, there was light enough for pistol shots.

At the agreed meeting place, a clump of trees not far from the Pré Catalan, the Comte de Bouttin, his two seconds and a doctor were waiting. The presence of a doctor was part of the ritual of a duel, for few of the many that were fought in Paris each year ended in anything more serious than a scratch or a flesh wound.

All six men were in black and wore top hats, but the comte had also put on a cloak which he had slung loosely over his shoulders. The cloak may only have been an affectation, a touch of theatre, but it seemed to invest him with an air of professional competence, the look of a man who had fought duels before and had every confidence in his own ability. His seconds bowed formally to Duthrey and Marigny when they climbed down from the carriage, but the comte turned his head away.

The comte's principal second drew Duthrey to one side and after a brief conference they returned. The other second then produced a flat, leather-bound box and when he raised the lid, Gautier saw lying on velvet a pair of duelling pistols.

'The pistols are already loaded,' the principal second told Gautier, 'and the choice of which one to use will be yours of course, Monsieur.'

The comte slipped off his cloak and both he and Gautier took off their hats and coats. Then the second who was carrying the pistols came forward to present them. As Gautier looked at the box, he suddenly began to wonder whether the choice he was being offered was as fair as it appeared. Because of the way in which the box was being held out to him, one of the pistols lay closer to him than the other. Could that mean that the nearer pistol was in some way inferior to the other, less likely to shoot straight, perhaps not even loaded at all? He was tempted to choose the further of the two pistols and then he thrust his suspicions aside. The gentlemen of Paris were too obsessed with what they saw as their honour even to think of such an ignoble deception.

He picked up the pistol nearer to him and the comte took the other. Then, as instructed by the principal second, they took up their positions back to back. At the word of command they began to walk in opposite directions; ten measured paces, slowly and with dignity. Then they would turn to face each other, raising the pistols and holding them at arm's length in the way Gautier had been taught at the Club des Mousquetaires. He already knew what he was going to do. The half-hour's target practice he had been given the previous evening after his abortive attempts to master the épée, had proved that he was unlikely to hit any target at 20 paces. So he had decided that he would let the comte fire first. Then, if he were still alive or only lightly wounded, he would fire his pistol into the ground or over his opponent's head. If anyone had asked him he would not have been able to explain his motives for this quixotic gesture, but that nevertheless was what he had chosen to do.

After walking ten paces, he turned and saw that the comte was already facing him. Could that mean that in spite of his outward calm the man was nervous and anxious to get his shot in first? Slowly, in unison, they raised their pistols and took aim. Although it was unlikely at that distance, Gautier thought he could see the comte's forefinger tighten on the trigger of his pistol. He stiffened his body and waited for the bullet. For an instant in his imagination he was St. Sébastien, waiting for the archers' arrows.

He heard an explosion which seemed to echo among the trees of the Bois, but no bullet came. Instead the comte's pistol appeared to disintegrate, surrounded by a bright flash of light, and with it his hand and forearm. The flash hid what would have been the changing expressions on the comte's face, surprise, horror, agony. As he collapsed, one could hear the beat of wings and the rustle of leaves as every bird within earshot flew up out of the trees in alarm.

When he reached the comte, the doctor, his brown bag beside him, was already kneeling over the injured man while his seconds looked down in shocked astonishment. The pistol had exploded, blowing off almost all of the comte's right hand and a fragment of metal had ripped through one half of his face. Gautier could not see for blood and mangled flesh whether the eye on that side of his face was still intact.

'We must get the comte to a hospital as soon as I have staunched these wounds,' the doctor said, pulling bandages from his bag.

Duthrey was white and, sensing that he was going to faint, Gautier reached out to steady him. The comte's principal second took Gautier's pistol and looked at it.

'You never fired, Monsieur,' he said, almost reproachfully.

7

JUDGE DUSSART WAS a persistent man, ready to repeat the same question in several different forms until he had an answer that satisfied him. It was this persistence that allowed him to carry out his duties as a juge d'instruction with at least some semblance of competence, for he lacked either the capacity for logical thought or any insight into human nature.

'Let us return, Mademoiselle,' he said to Miss Newbolt, 'to your reasons for going to your employer's room that morning. You have said that normally you did not go to her room until she was ready to take breakfast.'

'That is so.'

'Then why did you go down to her so early that morning?' Dussart looked at his notes. 'At between seven and seven-fifteen apparently.'

Miss Newbolt had already told the judge, as she had told Gautier on the day of the murder, that she had gone to Lady Dorothy's suite because for some reason which she could not explain, she felt something might be wrong, a presentiment that all was not well. Now she repeated her explanation, patiently and with composure, as she had answered all Dussart's questions. If the judge had hoped to bully or frighten her into a confession he was being disappointed, Gautier decided.

Next Dussart turned his attention to the money that had been found hidden in Miss Newbolt's room at the hotel. Through enquiries made at the bank which Lady Dorothy had visited on the day before she was found murdered, the police had established that the notes found hidden behind the wardrobe were those which Lady Dorothy had drawn against a letter of credit. In reply to Dussart's questions, Miss Newbolt could give no explanation of how the money had come to be there. All she could suggest was that whoever had killed Lady Dorothy must have hidden the money in her room to incriminate her.

'Who would want to incriminate you?' Dussart demanded.

'I have no idea.'

Although Dussart's questions then became openly hostile, accusing Miss Newbolt of taking the money herself from Lady Dorothy's room, she remained unruffled, repeating her denials calmly and without irritation. Gautier scarcely heard what she was saying for his mind had drifted back to the early morning. After the Comte de Bouttin had been rushed to hospital by his friends and the doctor, Duthrey, Marigny and Gautier had gone to the Ritz Hotel in Place Vendôme to take breakfast. They had planned the breakfast before as a celebration if Gautier should survive the duel, but when they sat down to eat, their mood had been sombre. Proud and arrogant though the comte was, they took no pleasure in thinking of his maiming injuries or the thought that he might even die.

'I still cannot understand,' Duthrey had remarked, 'why the fellow forced you to fight with him. He came to the café with that intention, you realize that?'

'Of course. Or why would his seconds have been waiting conveniently close at hand.'

'Has it occurred to you,' Marigny had asked, 'that what happened in the duel may not have been an accident? Perhaps you chose the wrong pistol, Gautier.'

The thought had occurred to Gautier and now, as Dussart nagged on with his questions, it returned to irritate him. The pistol might well have been tampered with so that it would explode when it was fired. But in that case, if the booby-trap had been intended for Gautier, some means would surely have been found to make him take or be given the pistol. On the other hand it seemed most unlikely that a handsome pair of duelling pistols, a collectors' piece, would have been allowed by neglect to deteriorate to the point when one would have exploded when it was fired. If both these alternatives were discounted, that left only one logical conclusion; whoever had tampered with the pistol had not cared which of the two duellists might be killed or injured.

When he forced himself to turn his attention back to the examination of Miss Newbolt, he realized that Dussart had switched back to questioning the Englishwoman on why she had gone down to Lady Dorothy's suite so much earlier than usual on the morning of the murder.

'You say you were worried in case something had happened to your employer?'

'Yes, that is correct.'

'And yet, even though you thought she might be in danger, you took time to dress before you went down?'

'I could hardly wander the corridors of the hotel in a dressing-gown.'

At precisely twelve o'clock Judge Dussart began collecting his papers together. Punctuality was another virtue with which he irritated all those who worked with him by demonstrating at every opportunity. 'That concludes my examination for the morning,' he announced. 'Gautier, please be kind enough to bring the mademoiselle back here at two this afternoon so we may continue.'

When Miss Newbolt and Gautier were outside the Ministry of Justice, he looked around him for a fiacre. The courts had already adjourned for the lunch recess and scores of lawyers streaming out into the street had quickly snapped up the fiacres which habitually waited by the Ministry.

'If we cross the river to the Right Bank,' Gautier told Miss Newbolt, 'we will surely find a fiacre and I'll take you to your hotel.'

'Unless you say I must, I would prefer not to go to the Cheltenham,' Miss Newbolt replied.

'Why is that?'

'Watching eyes, whispered remarks. Everyone, the guests as well as the staff of the hotel, know who I am now. Most of them have already decided that it was I who stabbed Lady Dorothy.'

'You exaggerate, Mademoiselle.'

'Do I?' She looked at him steadily. 'Do not the police also believe I murdered her?'

'I certainly don't,' Gautier replied and he realized that he meant it.

At first she said nothing, wanting to believe him perhaps, and fighting back her mistrust. Then she merely repeated, 'I would prefer not to go to the hotel.'

'In that case would you allow me to take you to lunch? I know a small restaurant not far from here which you might like, although it is unpretentious to say the least.'

She smiled and because the smile was unexpected it pleased Gautier. 'Are all French policemen as courteous as you are, Monsieur Gautier?'

'I would hope so.'

'And I am certain they are not.'

He took her to a small café restaurant in Place Dauphine, a tree-lined square only a few hundred metres from the Ministry of Justice. Until recently the café had been owned and managed by two women, a mother and daughter from Normandy. Janine, the daughter, had been Gautier's mistress until one day vitriol had been flung in her face. Although the scars of the attack had, through good fortune, been no more than mildly disfiguring, Janine and her mother had decided they could no longer endure the vice and violence of Paris and, selling the café, they had returned to Normandy. From time to time Gautier still ate at the café, mainly in the evenings because it was so conveniently close to the Sûreté, and also to enjoy the nostalgia of remembering Janine. She had been a pleasant, good-natured country girl, a virgin when they had first slept together who had grown to be as responsive and generous in her love-making as she was in everything else.

The new proprietors of the café, a middle-aged man with Italian blood from Nice and his wife, made Miss Newbolt and Gautier welcome. Gautier ordered sweetbreads and Miss Newbolt cassoulet and while they waited to be served, they ate chunks of crusty bread and drank from a bottle of light red wine from Provence.

'The cuisine here is usually good,' Gautier remarked, 'but simple. Not too simple for you, I hope.'

Miss Newbolt looked around the café with its plain wooden floor and wooden tables and the cheap lithographs on the walls. 'I'm delighted we came here. Whenever I travelled with Lady Dorothy—in France, Italy, Germany—what I wanted most was to go into ordinary restaurants, eat the food of the people and meet the people themselves.'

'And Lady Dorothy didn't want that?'

'No. She used to say she loved travelling but it was only her sort of travel, from Ritz to Ritz.'

Although Gautier was certain that Miss Newbolt had never before tasted such a simple, plebeian dish as cassoulet, she appeared to be enjoying it. He was surprised too at her appetite. The knowledge that she was suspected of having brutally and callously murdered another woman did not seem to affect her pleasure in eating and drinking and he admired her resilience. By contrast, he himself, in the shadow of Suzanne's death and aware of the likely consequences of his duel with the Comte de Bouttin, could only make a pretence of eating.

'How well did you know the late Earl of Tain?' he asked Miss Newbolt.

'Reasonably well. He used to spend a good deal of time in Lady Dorothy's house and he was always very friendly to me.'

'What sort of man was he?'

'Gentle,' she replied after a moment's thought. 'Gentle and kind and considerate. The servants loved him. But he was crushed by his wife and sister. Alice, the Countess of Tain, comes from a wealthy family and she never allowed him to forget that it was on her money that they were living.'

'And his sister?'

'Lady Dorothy doted on him. She had always been, and acted, the older sister, dominating him since they were young children. She said she distrusted his weakness. She and the countess formed an unholy alliance and between them they ran the poor man's life.'

As she was speaking, Miss Newbolt frowned, showing that her forehead and the corners of her eyes were creased by a mass of tiny wrinkles which, with her eyes themselves, gave her face an expression of haunting sadness. In not many years' time, Gautier reflected, the wrinkles would deepen and as the skin on her face began to sag, the sadness would be swallowed up in the ugliness of age.

'Forgive me for asking you this, Mademoiselle,' Gautier said, fearing that the question he was going to ask would shock a spinster who was also a priest's daughter. 'Do you have any reason for believing that the Earl of Tain might have had homosexual inclinations?'

'How did you know that?' Miss Newbolt asked sharply. She was not shocked.

'Know what? That he was homosexual?'

'No. What I mean was how did you hear about that business at his public school. I thought it was a family secret.'

'Tell me about it.'

At the age of 17 the Earl of Tain, Miss Newbolt told Gautier, had almost been expelled from his public school when some affectionate letters which he had written to a younger boy had been found by his housemaster. The affair, in her view, had been nothing more than a silly infatuation of a kind common enough among adolescents in the cloistered, unnatural surroundings of a boys' boarding school. There had been no evidence of homosexual practices and for that reason, after a good deal of influence had been brought to bear on the headmaster, the earl had been spared the ultimate disgrace of expulsion.

'His offence was forgiven but not forgotten,' Miss Newbolt concluded. 'He told me that from then on his family and especially his sister were always watching him, trying to keep him as far as possible confined to the company of women, looking out for any signs of perversion.'

'It's a wonder they did not drive him into it.'

'His mistake was to write letters to the boy; silly sentimental letters. But then the earl was incurably sentimental.'

'In what way?'

'Well, for instance, his love of rosebuds. He wore a rosebud in his buttonhole whenever he could get hold of one. And one day he told me it was because they reminded him of a girl he had known and loved years before.'

'Did he come to France very often, do you know?'

'Hardly ever. I believe his wife would not allow him to. He spoke good French and used to speak it to me as often as he could just for the practice, but he once told me that the last time he had visited Paris was in 1896. I believe he stayed for some time on that occasion.'

It struck Gautier that Miss Newbolt knew a good deal about the Earl of Tain which one would have expected him to have kept to himself. He would have liked to probe a little further and find out why a shy, elderly Scotsman should have been so ready to confide in his sister's companion, but he felt that to do so would be unfairly exploiting the fact that he was taking Miss Newbolt out to lunch. She would have questions enough to answer before Judge Dussart had finished his examination.

So he changed the subject and for the rest of the meal they talked of other things, mainly of France. Miss Newbolt's knowledge of French history and literature astonished him in one who had spent so little time in the country. She could only have acquired it by reading and he supposed that a lady's companion might spend a good deal of time waiting until her services were required, time which she could fill with reading. It would be a lonely life and Gautier wondered what effect that might have had on Miss Newbolt's temperament.

After they had finished their lunch they still had time to spare before returning to Dussart's rooms, so they walked back along Quai des Orfèvres and stopped for a time to look over the parapet at the river. On the opposite bank a man was fishing, an optimist, for the Seine had long since been fouled with the waste of manufacturing establishments further upstream.

'The other day you asked me if I knew why Lady Dorothy dismissed me,' Miss Newbolt said suddenly.

'Yes, and you told me you didn't know. That she lost her temper one day and told you that you were incompetent.'

'That was only partly the truth. I believe the real reason she dismissed me was that her brother left me a legacy in his will.'

'Why should that have annoyed Lady Dorothy?'

'Jealousy I suppose. On the other hand she may have decided that the earl and I had been having some sort of affair and that would have infuriated her.'

'One assumes that the legacy was not substantial. You told me the earl had no money of his own.'

'None to speak of. No, it was only about 1200 francs. Neither the countess nor Lady Dorothy knew about it until the earl's will was read.'

'He left you nothing else? No mementoes?'

'No. Nothing.'

They strolled back to the Ministry of Justice, stopping to look at the stalls of the bouquinistes as they went. At one stall Miss Newbolt picked up an old leather-bound volume of Pascal's

Pensées, opened it at random and began reading. Gautier could see that she was absorbed in what she read and he saw too that she could have no money with her for she was not carrying a reticule. So on an impulse he bought the book for her, handing the bouquiniste the few sous which he wanted.

She did not protest but accepted the gesture graciously. 'Thank you. Pascal will be a comfort to me in prison.'

'You are not in prison yet.'

'No and I am sure that I have you to thank for that.'

When they reached the ministry, Gautier found Inspector Lemaire waiting for him outside Dussart's office. Lemaire was a colleague at the Sûreté, good-natured but not very intelligent and harassed by a demanding wife. Gautier had often stood in for him on night duty, which may have been the reason why Lemaire appeared uncomfortable at what he had to say.

'I am to relieve you, Jean-Paul,' he said. 'On the director's instructions.'

'You are taking over the investigations into the murder of the Englishwoman then?'

'Yes. That is to say I am to be in attendance while the juge d'instruction carries out his examination.'

'And what am I to do?'

'Courtrand is waiting for you in his office,' Lemaire replied. Then he could not stop himself blurting out in a burst of sympathy, 'Everyone at the Sûreté knows about your duel. What on earth made you do it, Jean-Paul? Courtrand is mad with fury. This time he means to finish you!'

'I am sure, Inspector Gautier, that you do not need me to remind you of the gravity of your position.'

'No, Monsieur le Ministre.'

The Minister of Justice, François Godilot, was in his forties, a man with the short, stocky build and swarthy complexion to be found in the Midi. Once a practising lawyer, he owed his more recent success in politics not so much to his considerable debating skill as to his energy and competence. Less kindly people had even been known to suggest that the wealth and influence of his wife's family had also been an important factor in securing him a portfolio at such an early age, for while he came from a comparatively humble background, she had one uncle who was a cardinal and another who had been president of the Jockey Club. She herself was a small, determined woman who spoiled her husband and who, whenever she was not in the confessional, had an insatiable appetite for doing good works.

'If the Comte de Bouttin dies,' the minister went on, 'you may be facing criminal charges.'

'Even though I did not fire my pistol?'

'Can you prove that, Gautier?'

'My seconds and the other gentlemen present will testify that my pistol was never fired.'

'That was fortunate for you,' the minister remarked drily.

'Not really, Minister. You see I never intended to fire.'

The minister looked at Gautier and then at the Prefect of Police and at Courtrand; the look of a Minister of Justice, not a look of disbelief but one which, while it conceded that the prisoner must be given a fair trial, was nicely tinged with scepticism. Gautier could not help feeling that he was not so much on trial as already tried and sentenced. The fact that he had been brought before the Minister of Justice himself was surely proof that the severity of his offence had passed beyond the point when he might expect an impartial judgement. He had already spent half an hour in the office of the Director-General of the Sûreté, during which Courtrand's face had been stiff with a fury which he had only barely controlled. And when Gautier had admitted fighting a duel, giving details of the time and place, Courtrand had brought him to the Minister of Justice's office. There the Prefect of Police, now back from attending a conference in Brussels, had been waiting. The whole situation, the *mise en scène*, had been planned and, Gautier decided gloomily, the outcome already decided.

The minister seemed as though he were going to ask Gautier to expand on his last remark, but then he must have changed his mind, like a seasoned actor resists the temptation to improvise and returns to the script. He said, 'You have broken the law, Inspector; you who are supposed to uphold it. Surely you cannot expect such behaviour to be condoned?'

'No, Monsieur le Ministre.'

'I cannot say what the consequences of your foolishness will be at this point. Much will depend on whether the Comte de Bouttin dies. In the meantime you are suspended from duty.'

The minister leant back in his chair in the manner of one who had pronounced judgement and had nothing more to say. Then, changing his mind, he leant forward again and looked at Gautier severely. 'When I say you are suspended I mean exactly that. You have the reputation, Gautier, of being a difficult man, one who likes acting on his own impulses and who frequently ignores or deliberately misinterprets the instructions of his superiors. Let me make this clear. Until you hear from me again, you will keep well away from Sûreté headquarters and from your colleagues. Under no circumstances will you attempt to continue any investigations on your own account.'

The interview was over and Gautier left the minister's office accompanied by the Prefect of Police and Courtrand. That would not be the end of the matter, he thought wearily. There would be words, endless words, reproaches, indignation. Courtrand, obsequiously silent in the presence of the minister, would not be able to resist the delight of being able to remind Gautier of how many times in the past he had said that one day he would go too far, overreach himself, bring down the ignominy which his stubbornness deserved.

To his surprise, there were no words or reproaches, not from Courtrand at least. As soon as the three of them were outside the minister's office, the Prefect of Police said to Courtrand, 'I wish to speak with Gautier alone.' Then he turned to Gautier. 'If you would be so kind as to accompany me to my office, Inspector, we can talk on the way.'

The prefect was a tall, scholarly man who gave an impression of being no more than mildly interested in his responsibilities, but even junior police officers had sometimes learnt painfully that he had an astonishing insight into how efficiently or otherwise they performed their duties. He had let it be known more than once that he was impressed by the way Gautier had handled certain difficult criminal cases and his support had acted as a useful counterweight to Courtrand's open and loudly expressed disapproval of the not infrequent occasions on which one of his senior inspectors chose to ignore police procedure.

After Courtrand had left them, the prefect said, 'When I was told you had fought a duel, I would not believe it, Gautier. Then I heard of your wife's death. Please accept my deepest sympathy.'

'Thank you Monsieur, but that did not justify my behaviour.'

'Of course not. It is not an excuse but a reason. When we are deeply grieved we often act unnaturally.'

'I realize now that I should have known better.'

They walked in silence for a while. Gautier realized now that the Prefect of Police must have known for some time that his wife had left him and was living with another man. Some people might have resented what they would have seen as an intrusion by authority into their private lives. He was only grateful to the prefect for his discretion in not having shown before that he knew.

'Duels are being fought every week in Paris,' the prefect said presently, 'and we in authority turn a blind eye. It must seem unfair that you are being punished.'

'The minister was right. My duty is to uphold the law.'

'I tried to persuade him not to suspend you. The whole affair will be forgotten in a few days and after all you never actually fired a shot, but the minister is in a sensitive position.'

'In what way?'

'His wife is, as you know, a very religious woman and the minister himself is a strong supporter of the Catholic church. He owes his position to some extent to the backing of the clerical party. Obviously he could not be seen to be condoning any breach of morality and the reason for your being challenged to this duel appears to have been your association with a woman other than your wife.'

The prefect might also have added, Gautier thought cynically, that the woman was a widow still supposed to be in mourning. The hypocrisy of society would be quicker to censure a breach of its conventions than the immorality of illicit sex.

'What will you do?' the prefect asked.

'Do? Nothing, Monsieur.'

'Have you considered leaving Paris for a few days until we know the outcome of the comte's accident? By doing so you would escape the gossip and the slanders. Parisians can be very cruel.'

The notion that he might leave Paris had not occurred to Gautier, but as he thought about it he began to like it. With no work to do, life in Paris would be hard to endure. He would not be able to go to the Café Corneille, for this would embarrass his friends, and there could be no more clandestine evenings with Michelle Le Tellier. Having a duel fought over her while she was still officially in mourning for her husband would by now have already tarnished her name with scandal.

'I cannot help wondering,' the prefect continued, 'whether the duel was intended one way or another to kill you. You have made enemies you know, Gautier. Away from Paris you will be safe and in the meantime I will ensure that the whole matter is thoroughly investigated.'

8

A PALE, WEAK sun was doing its best to dispel the last traces of a sea mist which hung over the Channel, as Gautier walked along the promenade at Deauville. He walked quickly, with the impatience of a man tired of inactivity, who was ready to put his energy to work again.

He had chosen Deauville as a refuge for two reasons; mainly because it was not too distant from Paris, but also because he knew that a cousin of his former mistress, Janine, had a small pension in the town. The memory of Janine still troubled him and he had hoped that by staying in the cousin's pension he would get news of her. All he had heard was that she and her mother were well, living in the country and that there was talk in the family of Janine marrying a local farmer, a widower with three small children. The news had pleased him, easing as it did the guilt he still felt at knowing that it was because of him that she had been attacked and injured.

For three days after arriving in Deauville he had done nothing, passively immersed in the mood of depression which had seemed to take control of his life since the death of Suzanne. Then, unexpectedly, he had received a letter from his friend Duthrey. The main purpose of the letter had been to tell Gautier that the Comte de Bouttin was not dead nor dying, that he was recovering from his wounds, although he had lost the greater part of his right hand. In the circumstances, Duthrey was certain, no official action would be taken against Gautier and his suspension from duty would be lifted.

Gautier was not as optimistic as his friend, but another piece of information in the letter had caught his attention. Miss Newbolt, Duthrey reported, had been arrested and was being held in St. Lazare prison while her judicial examination continued.

The news of the Englishwoman's predicament had affected Gautier in a way that his own situation had failed to do. Without any sound or logical reason, he had come to believe that Miss Newbolt had not had any part in the murder of her employer and learning that she had suffered the indignity of being put in St. Lazare prison, a rambling and decrepit place with room for 12,000 prisoners, most of whom at any one time would be convicted prostitutes, where she might well stay for several weeks, had made him angry. It would suit the authorities for Miss Newbolt to be found guilty of a murder which had embarrassed them and they were not likely to make any strenuous efforts to establish whether she was innocent. And so indignation had provoked Gautier into trying to help her.

On receiving Duthrey's letter, he had travelled by train to Rouen and spent an afternoon looking through back numbers in the offices of the city's newspaper. It was 1896 that interested him; the year when, according to Miss Newbolt, the Earl of Tain had last visited Paris and had spent some time there. Something about the date bothered him and he had a feeling that something had happened in 1896 which he should remember. And so he had made a search of the newspapers on no more than a slender hope that it might give him an idea, a starting point for more fruitful enquiries. And once again, as had often happened in the past, his random venture had succeeded.

The year of the earl's visit, he had discovered, had been the year of the Flower Girl Affair and for several weeks the newspapers had carried lurid stories of the trial in Paris at which the Duc de Caramond and another member of the Jockey Club, a Monsieur Charles Bailly, had been charged with procuring three schoolgirls for sexual orgies. Sitting in the office of the newspaper, flicking casually through the reports it had published of the trial, Gautier had read that, in order to protect the three girls, their names had not been mentioned in court. Instead, the judges had allowed them to be referred to by names of flowers, the same names apparently as the duc and Bailly had given the girls in the course of their love games: Violet, Marigold and Rosebud.

Immediately, Gautier had felt a sharpening excitement. It was a single rosebud that had been engraved on the cigarette case he had found in Lady Dorothy's hotel room. Logic had told him that this might be no more than coincidence for Rosebud was not an uncommon name, but he had pushed logic on one side and trusted his instincts. Eagerly he had read every report of the trial in the paper and one article in particular, written on the day after the verdicts and sentences had been announced, was still fresh in his memory.

THE FLOWER GIRL AFFAIR

Nobleman and gambler found guilty and sent to prison

Finally, after a long, sordid and unnecessarily dramatic trial, the case of the so-called Flower Girl Affair ended with a verdict which to most of us had been a foregone conclusion. The Duc de Caramond and Monsieur Charles Bailly, well-known figures in Paris society, were both found guilty of corrupting the morals of young girls and both were sentenced to a term of five years' imprisonment. Satisfaction at knowing that these two monsters should have received the punishment that their depravity so richly deserves should not however blind us to the many disquieting features of the whole business. Questions remain unanswered. Three young girls were involved. Is it not likely there were also three men? If there was a third man—and this was openly hinted—who was he and how is it that he does not face trial with his vile companions? Why were the only witnesses, the girls themselves, not questioned on this point by the prosecutor? And again, who was the go-between who first brought these innocent girls and their seducers together? The girls were not known to the duc or Monsieur Bailly before they were led into the web of vice. Why was the procurer therefore not on trial? Some have praised the skill and oratory of the defence counsel in securing such a light sentence for his two clients. This newspaper prefers to ask how it was that such an ill-prepared case was allowed to come into court. Did someone use influence to make sure that awkward questions were not asked during the judicial examination? Was there corruption behind the scenes or was it just through lack of interest that the Advocate General conducted the prosecution so tamely and so ineffectively?

Continuing his search through the newspaper's library of back numbers, Gautier had been disappointed to find no further articles on the Flower Girl Affair in the weeks that followed the trial. He had hoped that, because of the interest which the affair had aroused, the paper's reporters would have looked for new stories with which to titillate the public's appetite for sensation: details of any other sexual indiscretions which the duc and Bailly might have committed, accounts of how they were enduring the discomfort of life in prison, of the home life and background of the three girls and later of what had happened to them. There was nothing and it appeared that the stir which the case had caused had soon faded.

Determined, before returning to Deauville, to follow the slender lead which he sensed that he had found, Gautier had spent another hour that afternoon talking to the journalists on the staff of the paper. Most of them remembered the Flower Girl Affair well and one had an interesting piece of information. About two or three years after the trial, he remembered, the paper had been told that one of the girls in the case, he could not recall which one, had started a career in the music halls and was making a name for herself, appearing under the name of Mimi La Belle.

Gautier had also learnt in Rouen that a well-known music hall comic, Achille Barbu, now retired from the stage, had settled in Deauville. Not long previously, the newspaper had published a feature on Barbu, recalling some of the highlights of the great comic's career and telling its readers how he was spending his retirement. Barbu, Gautier had been told, knew all there was to know about the music hall in France and if there was anyone who could help Gautier to trace Mimi La Belle, it would be he.

So that morning, after leaving the pension, Gautier walked along the promenade by the sea towards the residential part of Deauville where Barbu was living. The comic's villa was large and freshly painted and gave an impression of comfortable but unostentatious luxury. A maid let him into the house and he saw, hanging in the entrance hall and all the way up the stairs, framed music hall posters on most of which Barbu's name appeared in a prominent position. The maid led him to a study in which there were more posters and a number of fading photographs.

Barbu seemed to have changed very little since the last time

Gautier had seen him several years previously. He had then been performing not in a music hall but at the Eldorado, one of Paris's best known café concerts. He had an elongated face with a heavy jowl, clean shaven in spite of his name and a deceptive air of innocence. The most popular turn in his repertoire had been one in which he appeared dressed as a priest and told stories of grotesque incidents which he claimed had happened when he was ministering to his flock.

He greeted Gautier effusively, giving the impression that in his retirement, having lost his audiences of several hundred people, he was only too glad to welcome an audience of one. Finding out that the audience wished to hear about the music hall turned his pleasure into delight.

'I have performed in the capitals of the world,' he said. 'Paris, London, Berlin, Brussels, yes and even in New York. And I have appeared with all the great names, all the vedettes of the music hall. See!' He pointed to the posters and photographs on the walls around them. 'Dranem, Marius Richard, Marie Lloyd. Why, one night I found that I had to come on after the Petomane.'

The Petomane was the name chosen by a popular music hall performer with an unusual act. He was able to expel air from his anus at will and in doing so produced sounds of different pitch, combining them in rudimentary tunes. The audience, particularly women, would be convulsed with laughter at his antics.

'How would you like to follow the Petomane?' Barbu demanded.

'I wouldn't,' Gautier replied, 'except at a safe distance.'

He listened as the old man's reminiscences meandered on, following an erratic course through the fifty years of his music hall career. It was no hardship, for Barbu, unlike many comics, was as entertaining in conversation as he had been on the stage, a lively raconteur with a sharp sense of the ridiculous and a talent for vivid descriptions. He told Gautier how he had started performing in the café concerts where entertainment was provided only as a means of drawing in customers to eat and drink. The music hall, in his view, was the bastard child of the caf'conc', a place where people paid to be entertained and where food and drink, if they were available, were a secondary attraction. The caf'conc's were still a major force in the social life of the people of France but the music halls, more profitable to the impresarios, were gradually usurping them.

Eventually, much though he was enjoying Barbu's entertaining monologue, Gautier decided he must direct the conversation into a more productive channel. He asked the comic if he had ever heard of a music hall artiste named Mimi La Belle. At first the question seemed to disconcert the old man and one sensed that it would hurt his vanity to be asked a question about the music hall which he could not answer. Frowning, he ran his fingers through the few remaining strands of hair which he had plastered down on to his balding scalp with Brilliantine. It was a gesture which, on the stage, he had used to accompany a long joke about barbers. Then suddenly his frustration evaporated into a huge smile.

'For a moment you had me puzzled, Monsieur Gautier, but now I remember. I knew the young lady, but not under that name.'

'She had another name?'

'Marie Desjardins. That was the name under which she made her début as a chanteuse. Without too much success I fear. So she changed her act and began singing risqué songs and kicking her legs to show her frilly underwear.'

'And that was a success.'

'Much more so, particularly with foreigners. She was their idea of a naughty French ma'mselle. So she changed her name to suit her act and became Mimi La Belle. Now she appears mainly in music halls outside of France.'

'Have you any idea where she might be performing now?' Gautier asked.

Once more Barbu frowned and then brightened. 'It is just possible I may be able to help you, Monsieur. You see, I collect music hall programmes. Friends post them to me from all over the world.'

Rising from his chair he went and opened a large cupboard at the back of the study. The shelves of the cupboard were stacked with copies of music hall programmes. There must have been thousands of them, but they were neatly arranged, either by country of origin or in date order or both. In any event it did not take Barbu long to find the programme he wanted and he flourished it in front of Gautier, smiling.

'Here we are!' he exclaimed. 'Two weeks ago Mimi La Belle was on the bill of the Wilton music hall in London. I have little doubt she is still there.'

The theatrical boarding house in Camden Town, recommended by Barbu, in which Gautier took rooms for his stay in London, was owned by a widow, Madame Regine. If he could not have found lodgings with a Frenchwoman he would not have crossed the Channel, for he realized that with his sketchy knowledge of English he could never make any worthwhile enquiries on his own account. Madame Regine turned out to be a woman of about sixty who had been an actress herself and was highly articulate in her accented English, vivacious and amusing and helpful. With her assistance Gautier was able to confirm that Mimi La Belle was still appearing in London, but at the Essex music hall in Islington and not at the Wilton.

On the evening of his first day in London, Madame Regine took Gautier not to the music hall but on an expedition to Mayfair. The Running Footman in Hay's Mews was a public house used almost exclusively by servants of the families who had houses in and around Park Lane, Grosvenor Square and Berkeley Square. In its ambience, full of a cheerful, bawdy vitality, it was totally different from either the boulevard cafés or the little bistros in Paris where working people were to be found.

On their way there Gautier had told Madame Regine that he wished to find out anything he could about the family of the former Earl of Tain who lived, so he had been told, in an imposing house in Park Street. As soon as they arrived at The Running Footman she went to work, striking up a conversation with a group of men who were standing nearby. It was not difficult, for they were clearly fascinated by her French accent, heavily rouged cheeks and strikingly bright red hair. Gautier wondered whether they might be thinking that she was a lady of easy virtue, now retired. He could understand no more than a fraction of what was being said, but she appeared to be telling them salacious stories and soon a crowd gathered around her to join in the laughter and good-natured repartee.

After a time she drew Gautier on one side and told him in French, 'We are in luck, my friend. That woman is the cook of the Countess of Tain.' She pointed towards a plump, elderly woman who was sitting by herself drinking gin. 'I think it would be better if I spoke to her alone. But first buy me two glasses of gin.'

Gautier did as she asked. The few women in the public house, he had noticed, were almost all drinking gin while most of the men were drinking porter. He had bought himself a quart pot of porter for threepence and found it not at all to his taste, far heavier than the bocks he had sometimes drunk in brasseries in Paris.

Madame Regine took the two glasses of gin, sat down next to the woman in the corner and offered one of them to her. In a few minutes they were deep in conversation. The atmosphere in the bar was heavy with smoke from the clay pipes which many of the men were smoking. Rather than stay drinking on his own, Gautier decided to take a short walk in the fresh air while the two women enjoyed their gossip.

The streets in Mayfair were not much better lit than those in less prosperous parts of London and he found his way to Park Street precariously, avoiding the hansom cabs and horse-drawn omnibuses which still outnumbered the new motor buses. He was also passed by several automobiles and noticed that a great majority of them were of French or German manufacture—Mercedes, Renault, Daimler, Panhard—and remembered reading that English manufacturers had been held back in developing new models, because the Act of Parliament requiring automobiles to be preceded by a man carrying a red flag had not been repealed until 1896.

The Countess of Tain's house in Park Street was imposing, but not nearly as large or as lavish as a vast mansion owned by a brewer which stood not far away in Park Lane. Having seen the number of people who crowded into English public houses and noticed their extraordinary thirst for beer, Gautier was not surprised that so many brewers should have made great fortunes and been rewarded for their philanthropy with knighthoods or baronetcies.

As he passed the countess's house, the front door was opened and two women came out and climbed into a waiting carriage. One must have been about fifty, short and slight, and he supposed she must be the countess for he recognized the other as the remarkably pretty girl whose photograph he had seen in Lady Dorothy's hotel suite. Both were in evening dress and both wore diamond tiaras. In

French society no one would have dreamt of going out to dinner or the theatre so soon after the death of a sister-in-law or an aunt and Gautier wondered whether social conventions were less rigid in England or whether the Countess of Tain was deliberately ignoring them to divert attention from Lady Dorothy's untimely death.

He strolled back to The Running Footman and when he arrived found that Madame Regine was still talking to the Countess of Tain's cook. They were also still drinking gin but not, he suspected, the gin he had bought them. As he had not cared for porter, he decided to try gin himself and ordered a glass. The first swallow made him wince as the fiery, immature spirit burnt his throat. Nor did he like the sweet, oily flavour. He had heard that gin was the drink of the working people in England since it had been introduced to the country by William of Orange when he came from Holland to be king. Much had been written also of the drunkenness and misery which gin had caused and, tasting it, he was not surprised, for it could never be a drink to be savoured and enjoyed, but one to be taken only for the effect it might produce.

At last Madame Regine left the elderly cook and she and Gautier rode back to Camden Town in a hansom cab. On the way she told him what she had learnt of the Earl of Tain's family.

'The earl must have been a most sympathetic man,' she said, 'for all his servants loved and respected him. His wife, on the other hand, is hated. They say she is ambitious, grasping and cruel.'

'How many children have they?'

'Just the one daughter. The cook says she is to marry a prince of royal blood.'

'Did she mention Lady Dorothy Strathy?'

'Yes. The earl's sister. The cook says she died somewhere on the Continent recently.'

'Nothing more than that?'

'No, that was all she said.'

Gautier was disappointed. In his experience servants usually knew a great deal about their employers' private lives and often many secrets which they were not supposed to know. But he knew he had no right to expect that a few minutes' conversation with the Countess of Tain's cook would help him solve any of the puzzles surrounding Lady Dorothy's murder.

'The earl appears to have been very fond of our country,' Madame Regine observed.

'Why do you say that?'

'According to the cook he had a collection of books from France which he was always reading and he would speak French whenever he had the opportunity. That made him an eccentric in the eyes of the servant.'

'Did she say whether he visited France as often as his sister?'

'No. He would have liked to but his wife would not permit it.'

'I wonder why.'

'The cook thought she knew the reason. It seems that she has been in the service of the Tain family for almost fifty years, starting as a kitchenmaid in the household of the late earl's father. According to her, as a young man the earl was deeply in love with a lovely French girl of aristocratic birth. The girl's parents had been distantly related to the earl's grandmother and she would come to stay at his parents' home in London during the London season. There had been talk of a betrothal.'

But the earl's family, the cook had explained, had no money and nor had the family of the French girl. So, in order to preserve the Tain estates, a better match had to be found and the present countess was available. She was no beauty but her father owned a steelworks in the north of England.

Madame Regine raised her eyebrows and gave a half shrug of her shoulders, a gesture to show that she understood the practicalities of marriage. Gautier also understood them.

'Did the cook mention this French girl's name?' he asked.

'She only knew her christian name. And that was Arlette.'

The Essex Music Hall in Islington was one of the smaller and less well-known of London's music halls. Even so, in a short space of time after it had been built it had begun to attract a regular following from the working-class people in the East End of London and could now engage at least one of the famous artistes of the music hall to appear at each performance. On the night that Gautier went it was the comedian Little Tich. The tiny man with his large feet and mournful expression was by then an international favourite who had often performed in France.

The Essex, like most of the music halls in England, offered attractions beside those which the stage performances would give. Below the gallery was the promenade where prostitutes, brightly dressed and painted, paraded in search of custom. Music halls in England, as in France, had always been closely tied with this particular form of vice, although in recent years the authorities had been trying to sever the connection. Not long previously, two American visitors to the celebrated Empire in Leicester Square had been outraged when accosted by young ladies. A defender of public morals, Mrs Ormiston Chard, took up their complaint and when the Empire applied for a renewal of its licence, the Licensing Committee only agreed on condition that the entire promenade was abolished. The case became a cause célèbre, with protests and counter-protests and letters written to *The Times*, but virtue prevailed and the ladies could no longer ply their trade, or not at the Empire at least.

Gautier had established with Madame Regine's help that Mimi La Belle would be performing that night and when he took his seat in the Essex he studied the programme as he waited for the curtain to rise. Even with his limited knowledge of English he could understand the many advertisements which it contained: for Epps's Cocoa, Carey's Motor Repository, the Talbot Hotel in Cuckfield, Sulpholine skin lotion for pimples, Buchanan's Scotch Whiskies and Alf. G. Todd, the Anglo-American tailor.

The bill at the Essex that night was varied but uneven in quality. The antics of Little Tich roused the audience to convulsions of laughter and even though he could not understand many of the little comedian's jokes, Gautier shared their amusement, but several of the other acts—singers, a conjuror, clog dancers and a ventriloquist —lacked either vigour or polish. The audience, generous in its applause, was savagely cruel to any performer who failed to please and two of those who appeared that night left the stage to shouts of derision.

Mimi La Belle was not one of them. Plump and dark and vivacious, she seemed to match what the London cockney expected of a naughty French girl and although neither of the two songs which she sang were by any standards witty, it was enough that she sang them in a heavily accented English and lifted up her skirts coquettishly from time to time to show the frilly bloomers underneath.

When the performance ended Gautier went round to the stage door. Earlier that evening he had left a note at the theatre, asking Mimi if she would care to take supper with him after the show and including a letter of introduction which Barbu had kindly given him. At the stage door he found a note from her accepting his invitation and asking him to wait for her and presently she appeared.

At close quarters she was not as attractive as she had appeared on stage, for her features inclined to coarseness, but in spite of that the total effect was one of a provocative, sensual prettiness. She greeted Gautier with warmth and seemed glad to have an opportunity of speaking French. Even a music hall artiste, Gautier supposed, might from time to time be homesick.

In a hansom cab on the way to Romano's restaurant in the Strand, she asked him about Paris. She was not interested in either society or politics but in the stage and the caf'conc's and the music halls and more than anything in the well-known cocottes, the 'great horizontals' as they were often called: Caroline Otéro and Liane de Pougy and Emilienne d'Alençon. Mimi wanted to know about their latest exploits, the names and titles of the latest admirers, of the rivalry between Pougy and Otéro and whether King Leopold of the Belgians was still spending a large part of his private fortune on Alençon.

'Do you know, that is what I wanted to be,' she remarked suddenly.

'A cocotte?'

'Yes. Does that shock you?'

'No. Why should it?'

'What a wonderful life they have. Fine apartments, lovely clothes, jewels. Did you know that Otéro was bought a necklace which once belonged to Marie Antoinette? And Liane de Pougy was once paid 20,000 francs by a man just so he could see her naked, nothing more?'

'And you would prefer their life to acting?'

'Acting is hard work and poorly rewarded. Sometimes I must appear at two or even three different music halls in one evening just to make a living.'

Discontent passed like a shadow over her face and for a time she seemed to brood over the injustice of life. In Romano's she pressed Gautier to buy her champagne and they quickly finished a bottle, but it appeared to depress rather than uplift her spirits.

'I could have been a cocotte,' she said over supper. 'At one time everyone in Paris knew my name. My real name that is.'

'When was that?'

'Did you ever hear of the Flower Girl Affair?'

Her question solved a problem that had been occupying Gautier; and that was how he could steer their conversation round to Mimi's part in the celebrated scandal. He had not told her that he worked for the Sûreté, sensing that she might be reluctant even to dine with a policeman, and to have started during their first meeting to question her about an affair which had happened so many years ago must surely have seemed odd.

When he told her that he had heard of the court case, she said, 'Well, I was one of the girls; the one they called "Violet" in the trial.'

'Appearing in court must have been a great ordeal for a young girl,' Gautier commented.

'An ordeal? Not at all! The Presiding Judge was most considerate.' Mimi smiled. 'I believe the old scoundrel rather fancied me himself. Everyone was most sympathetic: the police, the journalists. By the time the case came to court I was only a few months under the age of consent. I had a number of offers from men who were prepared to wait.'

'But you refused them?'

'I was not given the chance to accept,' Mimi said indignantly. 'My parents were furious at what they thought of as the shame I had brought on the family. I was rushed away as soon as the trial ended, to stay with relations in the north. It was like a prison. Eventually I ran away, went to Marseilles and got an engagement singing in a caf'conc'.'

Gautier realized that Mimi had enjoyed what most people in Paris had believed was a harrowing experience for three young girls. She had liked the attention, liked what she no doubt saw as the lustful looks of male spectators in the court, liked seeing her photographs in the newspapers. They were all part of the life she would have chosen for herself had her parents allowed her to do so.

'What happened to the other girls in the affair?' he asked her.

'Noelle, the one they called "Marigold", was sent away to a convent by her parents. She died quite young of typhoid I believe.'

'And Rosebud?'

'She was different,' Mimi replied with a trace of contempt. 'A timid little thing. Simone her name was. Noelle and I enjoyed going to meet the men. For almost two months we saw them in this superb apartment every Monday afternoon. It had to be on Monday, for that was the only afternoon we could get away from school early without questions being asked. And the men were fun; amusing and kind and they gave us lovely presents which we had to keep hidden from our parents of course. But Simone never even wanted to come in the first place, only her family was poor and her mother sick. We had to find another girl so we persuaded her but she only came for the money.'

'How did you meet the men in the first place?' Gautier asked. 'Who arranged it?'

Mimi looked at him suspiciously and he realized that he was pressing her too far and too quickly. 'Some other man asked us if we would be willing to go to this apartment for some fun and we agreed just for a lark.'

'What man was that?'

'I forget his name. He was a servant I seem to remember. Or maybe he was just a pimp. Who knows?'

'At the time of trial didn't people say that there was a third man involved who was never brought to court?'

'There was no third man.' Mimi's answer was so prompt and so emphatic that Gautier realized she had been asked the question before, many times. He also realized from her change of tone that she was hiding something but he could not press her any further without revealing his interest in the matter, which he did not wish to do.

So he asked a different question. 'Do you know what happened to Rosebud?'

'I heard she married a grocer, a man named Decartier.'

9

WHEN THE TRAIN from Calais pulled into the Gare du Nord, Gautier was surprised to see Surat waiting on the platform. He had telegraphed from London to say he was returning to Paris and suggesting they might meet as soon as Surat could manage it, but by that he had meant in the evening when Surat came off duty. Courtrand, who believed in protocol almost as fervently as he believed in his own importance, would certainly disapprove of Surat having any contact at all with a police officer who had been suspended. If he knew that Surat had met Gautier at a time when he should have been working, he would be enraged.

'I doubt whether it was wise of you to come and meet me,' Gautier said while they were shaking hands, 'not in police time anyway.'

'It's all right, patron,' Surat replied seriously. 'I am working on a case in this district now and this is the time I normally would take my lunch.'

'What case is that?'

'The killing of a voyou from Marseilles who was found with his throat cut not far from here the night before last.'

'And how are things at Quai des Orfèvres?' Gautier knew that Surat would understand what he meant by the question.

'The Prefect of Police is carrying out an official investigation into how the Comte de Bouttin came to be injured.'

'And the comte?'

'They say that his condition continues to improve.'

'But I am still suspended from duty?'

'So I understand, patron.'

An official enquiry, Gautier knew, could continue for weeks, or even months and there was no guarantee that at the end of it he would not be dismissed from his position at the Sûreté. Surat may have guessed what he was thinking for he went on, 'If the prefect is taking his time over the enquiry it may mean that he hopes the excitement over your duel will eventually die down and that then you could be reinstated quietly and without fuss. He has always supported you.'

What Surat said was true and secretly Gautier had been hoping that the backing of the prefect might help him to escape the consequences of his folly in fighting a duel. He replied, 'Yes, but his powers are limited.'

'Everything will work out all right. The Sûreté cannot afford to do without a man of your ability.'

'You are no longer working on the murder of Lady Dorothy then?' Gautier asked, deciding that he should no longer bother Surat with his own problems.

'If you ask me, no one is working on the case at all.'

'What do you mean?'

As they left the railway station, crossed the forecourt and began strolling through the nearby streets, Surat explained what he meant. Inspector Lemaire was now in charge of the investigation but on the instructions of Judge Dussart he had abandoned any attempts to discover whether Lady Dorothy might have been murdered by an intruder or a thief. Dussart himself appeared to have finished his examination of Miss Newbolt, after questioning her at length and repetitively in a way which suggested that he hoped to trick her into a confession that she had murdered her employer. He had also questioned the hotel staff, but only in the most cursory manner and was now, as far as anyone could tell, doing no more.

'What about Lady Dorothy's jewellery?' Gautier asked. 'We know that was missing. Has nothing been done to trace it?'

'Not really. They have circulated a description of the pieces among jewellers, nothing more. It would seem that Judge Dussart believes that Miss Newbolt took the jewellery and hid it somewhere.'

'It would suit them if Miss Newbolt were proved to have stabbed her employer,' Gautier commented.

'When I told Lemaire about the enquiries you asked me to make at the Hotel de Lascombes, he wasn't interested.'

In the surge of events that had followed and in some ways overtaken Lady Dorothy's murder, Gautier had forgotten that he had asked Surat to go to the Hotel de Lascombes. 'What did you find out there?' he asked Surat.

'Nothing of any importance. No one could remember a titled Englishman ever having visited the place. But there was one odd thing, though.'

'What was that?'

'No one had ever heard of a Monsieur Decartier. Now if a letter had been arriving there every month for some years, one would expect that somebody would know the name, if only one of the hotel servants.'

'Perhaps the patron of the hotel told the servants to say nothing.'

They walked in silence for a time and Gautier began to wonder whether something might be troubling Surat. They had worked together for some years and the only times he had found Surat less than talkative had been when he was faced with a problem, often quite a trivial problem which he did not know how to handle. Today he sensed that if there was a problem, it might be connected with Surat's work and not with any family matter.

'Tell me about this case on which you are working,' he said.

'There is nothing to tell really. That's the trouble. We've established that the dead man's name was Mateer, that he was half African and that he was known to the police in the south as a pimp and suspected of dealing in drugs. So far no one we've questioned in the quartier admits to knowing him.'

'He may only have arrived in Paris recently. A good many of these voyous are drifting up here from the south.'

'Perhaps, but there's another thing which needs to be explained. We found several thousand francs in his pockets. Whoever cut his throat had not touched the money.'

Gautier hesitated, wishing to choose his words carefully so that if his diagnosis of Surat's uneasiness were wrong, he would not seem to be interfering. 'You seem unusually concerned over this business, old friend,' he said. 'Plenty of characters like this Mateer are murdered in Paris. Some people would say they are no loss to society.'

'I agree. They are no loss,' Surat replied. 'Nor is this Mateer, but this investigation is important to me personally.'

'Why is that?'

'As you well know, patron, the Director-General of the Sûreté has never thought highly of me. He thinks I am not intelligent enough for the work and too old.'

Gautier did not contradict Surat because what he was saying was true. Courtrand took every opportunity to criticize Surat's work and to draw attention to his shortcomings. He disliked the man mainly because of his unshakeable loyalty to Gautier, believing that only he and he alone was entitled to the loyalty of his staff. Now that Gautier was, for the time being at least, in disgrace, Courtrand was small-minded enough to bully Surat even more than he usually did.

'Things have been worse recently,' Surat continued. 'The director has hinted that I might be transferred to more routine work or even sent back to one of the police commissariats. But if I were to handle this murder case well, achieve something on my own. . . .'

He left the sentence unfinished but Gautier understood what he was asking. 'If I can be of any help,' he said, 'just ask me. I'll do what I can.'

'Would you really, patron?'

'Of course. You would be doing me a favour if you'd let me help. Remember, I have nothing to do and the days are long.'

He asked Surat a number of questions about the murder without learning much more than he already knew. Killings like that of the man Mateer were only too common in Paris and more often than not the motive for them was revenge; a pimp had stolen another pimp's girl or a thief had been cheated out of his share of a robbery or an informer had passed a message to the police about a large consignment of drugs that was changing hands. The people of the quartier, the petty criminals and their women, would almost certainly know who had been responsible for that knife slash in the dark alley, but they would not tell the police. Personal feuds had to be settled by their own code of justice, which had no need for the law. Surat would be fortunate indeed if he could extract any credit from a case like this one.

They discussed the case for a while and then Surat decided that it was time he continued with his official duties. He had been instructed to call at every café, shop and apartment within a radius of 250 metres of where Mateer's body had been found and to ask everyone to whom he spoke whether they had heard or seen anything on the night of the murder which might suggest a fight or a quarrel. Both he and Gautier knew that it was certain to be a fruitless operation.

After they had shaken hands and he had turned away down the street, Surat suddenly stopped, turned back and handed Gautier an envelope. 'I almost forgot, patron, this letter was delivered by hand for you at the Sûreté this morning.'

As he walked away, Gautier slit open the envelope. The letter inside was written on mauve notepaper headed with a coat of arms. The handwriting was elaborate, a succession of lavish curls and whirls joined by long, flowing curves, influenced by art nouveau no doubt, the handwriting of one who was less concerned with what was said than how it was presented.

Monsieur

A number of my friends will be joining me in my salon this evening. All of them would be delighted if you could be with us and some of them at least will, I am sure, be of interest to you. If you are free, may I have the pleasure of seeing you at nine-thirty?

Arlette de Nyren

Arlette, Gautier remembered, was the name of the Earl of Tain's first love, and he also seemed to think that he had heard of the name de Nyren before. He guessed that she must be one of the hostesses of Paris society who had soirées once or twice a week in their homes, to which they invited men of letters, politicians and musicians to mix with their friends from the gratin. The soirées in these salons had become an important feature of life in Paris society during the season, reported in detail by the newspapers, with hostesses like Madame Auberon and Madame Arman de Caillavet, the mistress of Anatole France, competing to persuade personalities like Clemenceau, Charles Maurras, Paul Hervieu, the philosopher Caro and the Italian poet d'Annunzio to join the ranks of their regular followers.

As Gautier put the letter away in his pocket he could not help wondering whether it was a coincidence that the invitation had arrived on the morning of his return to Paris, or whether Madame de Nyren had somehow found out that he was returning. Putting the thought out of his mind, he made his way by motor omnibus to St. Lazare prison in Rue Faubourg Saint Denis near the Gare de l'Est.

He was counting on the fact that his suspension from duty at the Sûreté would not be known to the prison staff and he was right. He had visited the prison many times before and they were not surprised when he told them that he wished to see the English prisoner Newbolt and he was shown into a waiting room while a warder went to fetch Miss Newbolt from her cell.

When she arrived he was astonished to find her looking exactly the same as when he had last seen her, calm and composed. Knowing the conditions in prison, he realized that she would have been herded together with the worst type of female criminals, thieves and drunkards, abusive and violent. It was a life calculated to degrade and he had expected to find Miss Newbolt if not dishevelled and distraught, then at least pale, unkempt and frightened. Instead, neat and demure, her hair beautifully brushed, she looked at him and smiled.

'Does this visit mean, Monsieur Gautier, that your interest in my situation has been rekindled?'

'My interest never abated, Mademoiselle, but unfortunately my superiors withdrew the case of Lady Dorothy's murder from my charge.'

'Why was that?'

'The reason was personal and in no way connected with the investigation.'

'You do not wish to tell me why?' Miss Newbolt still smiled but the question was a challenge.

'I have no objection to telling you.'

In as few words as possible Gautier told her of his duel with the Comte de Bouttin. When he had finished she said, 'I would never have thought that you would agree to fight a duel, no matter how much you were provoked. You surprise me.'

'I surprised myself.'

The room in which they sat was furnished with a wooden table and two chairs. It was mainly intended for the use of advocates who came to interview the prisoners they were defending and Miss Newbolt was sitting in one of the two chairs. She sat with her hands folded in her lap and Gautier was struck by her air of patience, not the patience of one resigned to whatever might happen to her, but of one who was indifferent to her fate.

'I was appalled to hear that they had brought you to this prison, Mademoiselle,' he remarked. 'St. Lazare is one of the oldest and worst of the prisons in France.'

'The conditions are dreadful, I admit, but the gaolers have been kind.'

'And the women with whom you share a cell?'

'One can only pity them.'

'How many of them are there?'

'We are seven in all, although if the cell were full it could hold nine.'

What she told him shocked Gautier. He knew that by paying only a few francs a day a prisoner at St. Lazare could get herself put in one of the so-called first-class cells which held only three women. He wanted to tell Miss Newbolt this but realized that perhaps she was without money. The thought that she might have been totally abandoned in this way by her English employers angered him.

'If you have been prevented from working, what have you been doing?' she asked him. 'One cannot imagine you staying idle for long.'

'I returned from visiting your country only this morning.'

'You've been to England! Whatever for?'

'To see if I could find out Lady Dorothy's reason for coming to Paris.'

He told Miss Newbolt about his visit to London, of Madame Regine's meeting with the Countess of Tain's cook in The Running Footman, of the evening he had spent at the music hall and of the dinner with Mimi which had followed. She listened without interrupting, but he noticed her frown more than once.

When he had finished she asked him, 'Do you believe Lady Dorothy's reasons for visiting Paris may be the motive behind her murder?'

'I am certain of it.'

She made no comment for a time, her frown now deepened to

furrows of concentration. Then she appeared to reach a decision. 'Monsieur, you have gone to a great deal of trouble and I believe you are doing it to help me. I will never be able to repay you but at least I owe you the truth.'

'The truth, Mademoiselle?'

'I told you once that my legacy from the Earl of Tain had been only a sum of money. That was not strictly true.'

'What more did he leave you then?'

'A packet. The reason I hid the truth from you is that the packet was left to me with a note asking me not to tell anyone about it.'

'And what was in the packet?'

'Nothing of any significance—or so it seemed to me at the time. It was a bunch of letters he had written to a French girl whom he loved.'

'Let me understand you,' Gautier said. 'If the earl still had the letters when he died, does that mean he never sent them to the girl?'

'That's correct. He explained in his note to me that he had written to the girl every year on her birthday but had never posted them for fear of compromising her. She was married you see.' Miss Newbolt smiled. 'I told you he was sentimental.'

'Then why did he leave them to you?'

'He wanted me when I was next in France to see if I could find a way of getting the letters to the girl discreetly. I brought the packet with me to Paris but unfortunately the earl gave me very little information that would help me trace the girl.'

'Did he not give you her address?'

'No. He said he did not know where she was living, but that I might find someone who did if I visited the Hotel de Lascombes.'

'And did you go there?'

'Yes, on the afternoon when Lady Dorothy was at the art exhibition. The earl said the girl was married to a grocer named Decartier. I spoke to a bald-headed man who appeared to own the hotel and explained what I wanted.'

'And what did he say?'

'That he had never heard of anyone by the name of Decartier.'

As he left the prison, Gautier felt, for the first time since he had heard of Lady Dorothy's murder, a sense of satisfaction. He had formed an impression of the late Earl of Tain as a kind, likeable and sincere man. Now what Miss Newbolt had told him confirmed what he had already guessed, that the money which the earl had been sending to Paris for so many years was the consequence not of a sordid, homosexual adventure, but of a romantic attachment to a young woman. Evil, as so often was the case, had existed only in the minds of others, in this instance the minds of his wife and his sister.

He was curious to read the letters the earl had entrusted to Miss Newbolt because, for no very logical reason, he believed that they must hold the key to Lady Dorothy's murder. Miss Newbolt had told him that on arriving in Paris she had placed the packet of letters together with her own modest jewellery in a safe deposit box at the Hotel Cheltenham. People with few material possessions, he had observed, valued them more highly than the rich who were accustomed to them. After some persuasion, she had agreed that Gautier might open the packet and had given him the key to the safe deposit box, which she had kept concealed in her clothes ever since she had been arrested.

When he arrived at the hotel and explained what he wanted, a young assistant manager led him to the strongroom where the guests' deposit boxes were kept. The whole of one wall of the room had been fitted with separate rectangular metal boxes, each one numbered and each of which could only be opened by using two keys, one held by the guest and the other by the management.

When Gautier handed him Miss Newbolt's key, the assistant manager produced the hotel's, opened the deposit box and took out a smaller metal box from inside it. He handed this to Gautier. In the box he found only three pieces of jewellery: a single string of pearls in a leather pouch, a diamond engagement ring still in its satin-lined box and a cameo brooch. Together with them was a small silver photograph frame with a faded snapshot of a handsome young man, dressed in the tropical kit of a British regiment and holding a solar topee under his arm.

'There is something missing from the box,' Gautier told the assistant manager.

'I know nothing of that, Monsieur.'

'Miss Newbolt left a packet in it as well, a bundle of letters.'

'If that is so, then the packet can only have been taken by the police.'

'The police?'

'An officer in plain clothes came here with an authority to search Miss Newbolt's belongings. Apart from him no one has opened the box.'

'How were you able to open the box for this man if Miss Newbolt still had her key?' Gautier asked.

'We hold duplicate keys to all the boxes.' The assistant manager seemed embarrassed by the question. 'It is necessary, you understand, Monsieur. Guests frequently lose their keys or leave taking them with them. Sometimes they have been known to die.'

'Were you present when this police officer opened Miss Newbolt's box?'

'No. He insisted on doing so alone.'

Putting the jewellery and the photograph back in the box, Gautier returned it to the assistant manager to lock away in the strongroom. There was nothing more to be learnt from them but, although the path he had hoped to follow was blocked, he felt neither depressed nor frustrated. Other paths, other lines of enquiry would open up and at least he knew now that the Earl of Tain's letters were important enough for them to be impounded.

Almost as an afterthought, he asked the assistant manager one final question. 'I suppose you did not notice who signed the letter of authority which this police officer showed you.'

'Of course, Monsieur. I checked it before I agreed to open Miss Newbolt's box. The authority was signed by the Prefect of Police.'

On his way out of the hotel, Gautier stopped at the concierge's desk. The concierge was there, fulfilling the requests of the guests with unshakeable efficiency, sending out pages to fetch tickets to the opera for the Germans, to book tables at Maxim's for the Americans, to buy bicarbonate of soda for the English, whose stomachs seldom seemed robust enough for the combination of French cuisine and Paris water. Gautier waited for an opportune moment to ask him a question.

'I wonder, Monsieur, whether by any chance you know of a Madame Arlette de Nyren?'

'But certainly!' The concierge seemed glad of an opportunity to demonstrate his knowledge. 'Madame de Nyren comes of an old and highly respected family.'

'But it's not a French name.'

'She married a Dutchman, the owner of a shipyard who died some time ago. Her maiden name was Arlette de Caramond.'

'Is she related to the Duc de Caramond?'

'Yes. She is his only daughter.'

'Was the duc once involved in an unfortunate scandal?' Gautier put the question as tactfully as he could.

'That is so.' The concierge leant forward to reply, lowering his voice as though he disliked to have such a shameful episode even mentioned in his hotel. 'The duc was sent to prison for his part in the Flower Girl Affair.'

10

MADAME ARLETTE DE NYREN lived in an apartment in Boulevard de Courcelles overlooking Parc Monceau, in a district of Paris which was becoming increasingly popular among the wealthy bourgeoisie. They preferred the modern apartment buildings which were being built there to the narrow streets and the, for them, stifling atmosphere of the Left Bank between the Sorbonne and Quai d'Orsay, which was where most of the remaining aristocratic families, Le Monde, still lived.

When he arrived at the apartment that evening and was taken by a manservant to meet his hostess, Gautier was not surprised to find her dressed all in white, with a long, shapeless white dress which, with only slight alteration, would have served as a shroud, and a white band around her forehead. From the middle of the band above her eyes, an enormous jewel, vulgar enough to be a genuine ruby, blinked like a red searchlight at those who had the courage to stare at it. An hour spent that afternoon in the offices of *Figaro* flipping through back numbers of the paper which Duthrey had made available, had taught him that Madame de Nyren's reputation in Paris society was based on her eccentricity. The gossip columns told of how she slept with a three-foot crucifix above her head in a bedroom without windows and with walls lined with cork, of the baby alligator which shared her bath and of how once, disguised as a man, she had been admitted to a very special bordello where the Prince of Wales was being entertained.

At her soirée that evening she greeted her guests sitting in a bamboo chair that had been encrusted with diamonds. As she allowed Gautier to kiss her hand she said to him, 'I am glad you recognized your obligation to me, Monsieur, by coming here tonight.'

'What obligation, Madame?'

'You have deprived me for the time being at least, of the devotion of one of my most faithful followers, the Comte de Bouttin. It is only fitting that you should take his place.'

To have told Madame de Nyren that it was not he who had wounded the comte would have been pointless so Gautier inclined his head and replied, 'I shall do my best, Madame, to console you for his absence, but I am certain my attentions could never be as welcome as the comte's.'

She tapped him playfully on his arm with the fan she was carrying folded in her hand and smiled flirtatiously. 'One never knows, Monsieur. One never knows.'

More guests arrived to be greeted in their turn and Gautier moved away. Although the drawing-room of the apartment was not large, it had been decorated in the style of art nouveau which was then becoming fashionable and, to match the lavish flowers and leaves and curling tendrils in the fabrics and the wallpaper, the room had been filled with plants in huge pots and armfuls of flowers in Chinese vases. These, combined with paintings that crowded the walls and an extraordinary assortment of ornaments which occupied every square centimetre of space on the mantelpiece and bookcase and grand piano, made the room seem suffocating.

Some thirty people were already assembled for the soirée and among them Gautier recognized a young poet, a protégé of his friend the bookseller Froissart, whose first volume of verse had been extravagantly praised, a handsome Brazilian woman who was reputed to be the leading figure in a colony of lesbians and Juliette Prévot, an author with whom Gautier had once shared a brief affair and who, after many disappointments, had at last been awarded the Prix Femina for her salacious, witty novels. When Juliette saw Gautier she beckoned him over to her.

'Jean-Paul! So you are invading the social scene again! That means trouble for some poor unfortunate, one supposes.'

'Not at all. I came in answer to an unexpected invitation from our hostess.'

'If she invited you it means you have become a celebrity. I wonder why.' Juliette frowned thoughtfully and then smiled. 'Of course! That infamous duel! I have to say, Jean-Paul, I was astonished to hear that you had wounded the Comte de Bouttin in a duel with pistols.'

'Astounded that I should be capable of wounding him?'

'Don't be flippant! Astounded that you should do anything so out of character as fighting a duel.'

'It may be a delayed effect of your influence. You were always telling me that my life was too dull, too prosaic, lacking in adventure.'

What Gautier said was true. During their time together Juliette had often reproached him for his orthodoxy in observing the conventions of bourgeois morality and its code of behaviour. He had accepted her taunts with good humour, but had never been provoked into following the daring suggestions she had sometimes made.

'Are you in serious trouble for fighting the duel?' she asked him and he knew she was concerned.

'In trouble, yes, but how serious remains to be seen.'

'Would it help if Madame de Nyren interceded on your behalf with the Prefect of Police?'

The question puzzled Gautier. 'Why should she?'

'The prefect is one of Arlette's most devoted admirers.'

'You cannot be serious!'

The Prefect of Police had never struck Gautier as being the type of man who would move in the same social orbit as Madame de Nyren. Although the salons of hostesses like Madame de Nyren had literary pretensions, the conversation to be heard in them was for the most part frivolous gossip and one could find more wit and learning in the boulevard cafés. The prefect, one would have thought, was too serious and responsible a man to enjoy the flirting and the chatter and the occasional scandals of the drawing-room. On the other hand, Gautier knew that he had been a widower for some years and had no children. It might be that loneliness had overcome his judgement.

'People say that she has been his mistress,' Juliette replied, 'and that he still adores her. She was thought to be a great beauty once, you know.'

'So I understand.'

'And he's here tonight.'

Juliette was right. Gautier had not noticed the prefect among the throng of people in the room but Juliette pointed him out, standing in a far corner and talking to a tiny man with white hair. The old man was a Norwegian living in Paris, the philosopher Kristofferson, celebrated for his ability to stun any audience into a paralysis of boredom with long dissertations on the minutiae of his enormous knowledge.

Juliette chattered with Gautier a little longer and was then kidnapped by the Brazilian woman, who led her away on the pretext that she must meet a new arrival, also from South America, the wife of a wealthy rancher. Gautier wondered whether Juliette's novels, all of which were passionate in their support of the rights of women, may have misled the Brazilian into believing that she might be a potential recruit for her lesbian colony. If so, he could have told her she was wasting her time.

Elbowing his way as best he could through the growing crowd of guests, he went over to the Prefect of Police, who seemed relieved to be rescued from the philosopher but embarrassed to find Gautier at the soirée. 'I did not know you would be returning to Paris so soon,' he remarked with a hint of reproach.

'I arrived back only today, Monsieur le Préfet,' Gautier replied and then, to forestall another question, he added, 'And I found an invitation from Madame de Nyren awaiting me.'

'It surprises me that she should be holding a soirée this evening. Her old father is seriously ill you know.'

'That is the Duc de Caramond, is it not?'

The prefect looked at Gautier sharply. 'Yes. Why, do you know him?'

'Only by reputation.'

After a short time the philosopher disentangled himself from them and went in search of a more admiring and less talkative audience. As soon as they were alone Gautier asked the prefect, 'May I ask what progress you have made in your investigation, Monsieur?' The prefect seemed not to understand the question so he added, 'You recall you said that you would have the matter of how the Comte de Bouttin came to be wounded thoroughly investigated.'

The prefect seemed almost to flinch at the question. In theory,

Gautier should not have asked it but he had been counting on the favours which the prefect had appeared to show him in the past. He found himself wondering whether anything had happened to change the prefect's attitude.

'You must not expect quick results, Gautier. An investigation like the one I am conducting takes time. All those who were present at the duel have had to be questioned. The pistols must be sent to laboratories for testing. It may be weeks before we know with any certainty what happened that morning and who was responsible.'

'I understand, Monsieur.'

'You may be assured that we are moving as fast as we can. I am conducting the enquiry personally.'

'Thank you. That is good to know.'

Neither of them spoke for a time and the prefect seemed uneasy, like a man with bad news to impart who had decided to hold it back. The constraint between them was so uncomfortable that it came as a relief to Gautier when Madame de Nyren brought all conversation to a halt with an announcement. She introduced an Italian pianist, a newcomer to France but a musician who, she declared, was certain to achieve fame within the next few months and who would now play one of his own compositions. The recital was short, mercifully, because there were not enough chairs in the room to seat more than a handful of those present, but it was long enough for the Prefect of Police to leave Gautier's company without having to give an excuse.

After the music ended Gautier had an unrewarding conversation with a middle-aged couple, almost as eccentric as their hostess, who told him with some pride that they had shocked the guests at their daughter's wedding by arriving at the church on bicycles and wearing cycling bloomers. Then, escaping from them, he was lectured by a banker, a collector of paintings, on the impudence of Picasso, Utrillo and the other avant-garde artists up in Montmartre for daring to pretend that their meaningless daubs were art.

By the time the lecture had been concluded, Gautier noticed that a number of Madame de Nyren's guests were starting to leave and he decided that he too might bring to an end what he now recognized had been a wasted evening. But before he could put his decision into effect, he saw his hostess crossing the room towards him.

'Monsieur Gautier,' she exclaimed, holding her hands out towards him so that he did not know whether he was supposed to kiss them or to grasp them affectionately. He did neither and she continued, 'I am enchanted that you are still here! We must have a little chat, that is if you can spare the time.'

'I am at your disposal, Madame.'

'Then let us go out on to the balcony where we can be in peace.'

The apartment was on the first floor of the building and from the drawing-room double glass doors led on to a balcony which overlooked Parc Monceau. The evening was warm enough for Madame de Nyren to brave the fresh air with only an embroidered silk shawl to cover her shoulders, neck and throat, which had been left generously exposed by the very décolleté dress she was wearing.

'Tell me,' she said when they were alone on the balcony, 'what horrid crime are you investigating at the moment?'

'None. I have been suspended from duty on account of the duel.'

'Really? That seems unreasonably harsh. Then what were you doing before you were suspended?' Madame de Nyren smiled and rolled her eyes with a comic pretence of horror. 'You must forgive my curiosity, Monsieur, but crime fascinates me, the fearfulness of it, the violence, the blood!'

'I was investigating the death of an Englishwoman in one of our leading hotels.'

'Lady Dorothy Strathy? Of course! I read all about it in the newspapers. They are saying that her companion stabbed her. Do you believe that?'

'Possibly. In any event she has been arrested.'

'I knew Lady Dorothy some years ago.'

Although Madame de Nyren was volunteering information, Gautier suspected that her whole point in inviting him to her soirée that evening and then taking him out on the balcony to talk was to find out how much he knew about Lady Dorothy's murder. That might be mere curiosity or she might have a more devious motive. The only way of discovering what she had in mind was to play the game she had begun, but to play it more skilfully than she.

'You also knew her brother the late Earl of Tain, did you not?'

'Yes. He was an old friend.'

'They say that you almost married him.'

'Who told you that?' Madame de Nyren did not seem surprised at the question. 'The Countess of Tain?'

'I have never met the countess. No, I heard it at secondhand from one of her servants.'

'It's true.' Madame de Nyren paused, as though she were savouring the nostalgia of her distant romance. 'I might easily have become the Countess of Tain, instead of plain Madame de Nyren.'

'But your families decided it was not a suitable match?'

'Yes. His had no money, nor had mine. So in the end we both had arranged marriages. It was sensible, but sad.' She sighed. 'I wanted to remain friends and we corresponded for a time, until Lady Dorothy put an end to that.'

'Lady Dorothy? Not the countess?'

'No. The poor earl was completely dominated by his sister and she hated me. Do you know she visited Paris scores of times but never once came to see me.'

Gautier recognized the remark, thrown out seemingly at random, for what it was, a subtle probe deliberately testing his knowledge. He decided it would do no harm to reveal at least a part of what he knew. 'But you saw the earl, I suppose, when he came to Paris in 1896?'

'Yes, he was a guest in my home. His sister did not want him to come but for the first and probably the only time in his life he defied her and that awful wife of his.'

'He stayed in Paris for quite a time, I understand.'

'About a month.' A look of discontent clouded Madame de Nyren's face and she added sulkily, 'He spent most of his time with that dreadful old roué, the Duc de Narbonne.'

'The duc was well known as a pédé, was he not?'

'He still is, even though he's almost eighty. My father was a good friend of his wife the duchesse. What stories she told about him!'

Madame de Nyren began recounting the stories she had heard from her father about the Duc de Narbonne. Gautier realized that she had deliberately but adroitly changed the conversation. He wondered whether she had done so because she had found out what she wished to know or whether she felt that his questions were moving into a dangerous area. Presently they returned to the drawing-room to join Madame de Nyren's other guests.

On the way she remarked, 'Looking at me now, Monsieur Gautier, you must be wondering why the Earl of Tain was so much in love with me.'

'Not at all, Madame!'

His reply was more than mere gallantry. Although Madame de Nyren's face was lined and she seemed to have developed a squint, one could still detect traces of her earlier beauty, just as purity of line and harmony of composition can still be discerned beneath the darkened colours and flaking paint of an old masterpiece.

'I have had many lovers. Just before he died my husband complained that he was the premier cocu of France. He was joking of course, but not entirely.'

'I am sure the reports of your infidelity were greatly exaggerated,' Gautier replied, sensing that this switch to coquettishness was for the benefit of the others in the room.

'Gracious, I hope not!' The ruby in Madame de Nyren's headband seemed to wink as though to complement her coy smile.

A short time later when Gautier made his excuses and left the soirée, he noticed that the Prefect of Police was still in the room, standing in the background patiently like a specially favoured guest who knows that he is expected to wait until the others have gone.

Before he kissed his hostess's hand, Gautier asked one last question: 'What was the purpose of the Earl of Tain's visit to Paris when he stayed with you, Madame? Was he here on business?'

Madame de Nyren's reply came promptly, showing that she had been expecting the question. 'Heavens no, nothing like that! It was a purely social visit, just to see an old friend.'

11

SPREAD OUT ON the table in Gautier's living-room, the possessions which had been found on the body of Mateer seemed a pathetic reminder of man's mortality. Apart from the bundle of money which the man from Marseille had been carrying and which was now locked away in a safe at Sûreté headquarters, his pockets had offered no more than impersonal, commonplace objects which gave no clue to his personality or his habits or his style of life: a stained and crumpled handkerchief, a comb, three toothpicks and a small tin box which could have been used to keep anything from buttons to throat pastilles but was now empty.

'I can understand your difficulties,' Gautier told Surat. 'On this evidence the dead man is completely anonymous.'

'I agree, patron.'

'Too anonymous if you ask me.'

When he had suggested that Surat should bring the dead man's possessions over to his apartment, Gautier had meant simply the objects that he had found in his pockets. One could often learn a great deal from the assorted bric-a-brac which most men carried around in their pockets and he had in mind that he and Surat should examine them together. But Surat, typically, had taken the suggestion literally and brought the clothes which Mateer had been wearing as well in a small valise. Since the contents of the dead man's pockets told them nothing, they took the clothes out of the valise.

They consisted of a double-breasted black suit, a white shirt and a stiff collar, a tie and a black bowler hat; not the clothes a working man would have worn. On the other hand neither did they conform with what a bourgeois office worker or minor civil servant would have chosen, for convention demanded that both of these should wear a frock coat. Underwear and socks were ordinary enough, but Mateer had been wearing shoes and not boots, which again seemed unusual for a man of his social station. In addition to what he had been wearing, a bow tie had been found in one of the suit's pockets and Surat showed it to Gautier. It was a ready-made black tie of the type worn by waiters in restaurants and cafés. None of the clothes, although in need of pressing, looked well-worn and Gautier judged that they might have been purchased within the last week or so.

The bowler hat in particular looked new. Almost without thinking, Gautier felt inside the band which ran around the inside of the hat and found that it had been padded with a folded strip of newspaper. It was a common way of making a hat fit when it was half a size too large for the wearer. Opening out the strip of newspaper, he saw that it had been torn from a Marseille daily paper that had been printed ten days earlier.

'It would seem that our friend was a newcomer to Paris,' Gautier remarked, 'and that he bought these clothes especially for his visit.'

'Where do you suppose he would have been staying? With friends?'

'That's unlikely. The kind of friends a voyou like that would have would not be living in homes with guest rooms.'

'A hotel then?'

'Yes. One of those cheap hotels around the main railway stations and most likely near the Gare de Lyon, if he came from Marseille.'

'We can start making enquiries around there.' Surat could not suppress the disappointment in his voice. A door-to-door tour of the hotels where Mateer might have stayed would take days.

'You've searched the clothes thoroughly I suppose.'

'I've been through all the pockets and felt the lining of the suit for any papers he might have concealed there, but I found nothing.'

'Pass me the shoes.'

Taking each shoe in turn, Gautier first peered into and then felt inside it. The inner sole of the second shoe seemed loose and when he lifted it up, he found underneath two pink pieces of card. Each piece was numbered and on the back of each was printed the name P. Berthier et Fils. Gautier recognized them at once as pawn tickets.

Without the scores of pawnbrokers in Paris, poor people would not have survived. When times were bad they would pawn almost anything they possessed, including their clothes, to raise money. In spring many families regularly pawned their blankets, hoping to earn enough in summer when work was plentiful, to be able to redeem them from the pawnbroker before winter set in again.

'Strange!' Gautier commented. 'Our friend has new clothes and a bundle of money in his pocket and yet he has been pawning things.'

'Maybe that was how he got the money to buy the clothes.'

'I doubt it. Pawnbrokers don't usually advance sums as large as that.'

'We could find the pawnshop, but that would take time.'

'Not necessarily. Two or three years ago, with the help of the police in every arrondissement, we made a list of all the pawnshops in the city. I believe I have a copy of the list here in my apartment.'

Gautier found the list without difficulty. His wife Suzanne had been an orderly girl and to make the best use of their small apartment, she had found a place for everything and everything was kept in its place. The discipline of tidiness she had introduced had survived after she left Gautier and was continued by the woman who came in to clean the apartment. Although there were more than 300 pawnshops in Paris, Berthier was not such a common name and they found P. Berthier's establishment listed against an address in the tenth arrondissement.

'If you leave the tickets with me, I'll take them to the pawnshop and find out what Mateer pledged there,' Gautier suggested.

'I'll come with you.'

'Will not your family be expecting you at home?'

'This is more important.'

Surat had a wife and four children and since, like most of the police officers at Sûreté headquarters, he worked twelve hours or more a day, the only time he spent with his family was on the days when he was not on duty. Even so Gautier knew better than to try and dissuade him and they made their way together to the tenth arrondissement by one of the new motor buses.

Berthier's establishment was much like the other pawnshops in Paris and Berthier himself was a stout man with large moustaches and a heavy silver watchchain draped across his waistcoat. He sighed when Gautier produced the pawntickets and explained that he and Surat were from the Sûreté. He was as honest as one might have reasonably expected any man in his profession to be and did his best to avoid handling stolen property but, as he often explained to the police, he had a living to make and was not gifted with second sight. He checked the numbers of the pawntickets against entries in a ledger of his transactions.

'Each ticket was for one item of jewellery,' he said presently. 'You will wish to examine them I assume.'

'Yes, but tell me, how much did you advance on them?'

'Twenty francs on each.'

'Then they were almost worthless,' Surat exclaimed.

'Not necessarily.'

'But if the jewellery was valuable, surely he would have asked for more?'

'That depends. If the items were stolen the thief might only wish to leave them here for a short time. A pawnshop is like a safe deposit to a criminal. He can leave stolen goods here until the robbery is forgotten and then redeem them and sell them. That way he can get a much better price.'

Leaving Gautier and Surat at the counter, Berthier went into the back of his shop and returned shortly with two brown paper pouches. When he opened the pouches and held them upside down, a gold ring and a locket fell on to the counter. The ring, a signet ring, was engraved with a coat of arms and when Gautier opened the locket, they saw inside it a miniature portrait of a young boy with fair hair curled in ringlets wearing a velvet suit.

'Unless I'm mistaken,' he told Surat, 'this is the jewellery that Lady Dorothy brought with her to Paris.'

'Old friend, it is good to see you again.' Duthrey shook Gautier's hand warmly.

'I am glad to be back in Paris.'

'You should never have left. You have nothing of which to be ashamed, no reason to hide. Your friends at the Café Corneille have missed your company.'

'I kept away to spare them embarrassment.'

'Embarrassment? What nonsense!' Gautier could not remember Duthrey ever speaking to him with such familiarity. Their friendship, although close, had always kept within the strict bounds of that formality so respected by the bourgeoisie in France. Since Duthrey had acted as his second in the duel, though, their relationship appeared to have become perceptibly more intimate. 'Come to the Corneille,' Duthrey continued, 'and you will find that your friends will greet you with sympathy and respect. In that business of the duel you behaved with much honour.'

They had met in the offices of *Figaro*, where Gautier had come from Berthier's pawnshop after sending Surat home. Surat had not wished to go but Gautier had insisted that he at least had his lunch with his family and they were to meet again in the afternoon. Duthrey shared a room at the newspaper's offices with four other journalists and they had found privacy in the library where back numbers of the paper were kept filed. It was a gloomy, airless and musty room, not inappropriate, Gautier thought, as a resting place for scandals long dead and the remains of so many reputations.

'It is about the duel that I wished to speak with you,' he told Duthrey, 'or to be more specific about the Comte de Bouttin's two seconds.'

'What about them?'

'Do you recall their names?'

'Yes, I still have their visiting cards. One was a Monsieur Léonide Raspail and the other a Monsieur Jean Fosse. Why?'

'Do you know anything about either of them?'

'A little,' Duthrey replied. 'I was inquisitive enough to find out what I could. I reasoned that if one of the pistols had been tampered with, it could only have been done with the collusion of those two gentlemen.'

'And what did you learn?'

'Raspail is an old friend of the comte and well known in society; one of those young rakes now approaching middle-age who will not shake off their wild ways. But the strange thing is that I could not discover anything at all about Fosse. No one to whom I mentioned his name had ever heard of him.'

'That isn't impossible. Paris is a huge city.'

'Yes, but here's an even stranger thing. I persuaded one of the young men who works for us to make discreet enquiries at the address given on Fosse's visiting card. No one had any knowledge of him there either. In fact the address is not one of a house or apartment building. It is a working man's bistro with a brothel above.'

'Was it not Fosse who held the pistols out for me to choose one?' Gautier asked.

'It was. My impression is that it was he who had brought the box of pistols with him. Raspail never handled them at all.'

'Can you remember what happened to them after the duel was over?'

'The pistols? No. In the excitement, with the comte lying on the ground wounded and in danger of bleeding to death, I never noticed. Later it struck me that we ought to examine the pistol you chose, just to check that, as Raspail said, you did not fire it, but both the pistols and the box they were in had vanished.'

'As had this Monsieur Fosse, no doubt.'

'Yes. You may recall that he left before anyone else while the comte was still being treated by the doctor.'

Gautier had not been able to remember exactly what had happened after the Comte de Bouttin had collapsed, bleeding. He had a vague impression of watching the doctor kneeling over the wounded man and tying a tourniquet high up on his right arm and then of a horse-drawn ambulance arriving. He could barely remember even the breakfast which Duthrey, Marigny and he had taken at the Ritz Hotel nor of what they had talked while they ate.

'I suppose you have been asked all these questions already?' he said to Duthrey.

'No. Why should I have been?'

'The Prefect of Police has been carrying out an investigation into how exactly the Comte de Bouttin came to be so seriously injured.'

'Well, no one has approached me on the matter, nor Marigny either.'

By mid-afternoon Gautier and Surat had learnt a good deal about Mateer. Finding the pawn ticket had punched a small hole in the dead man's anonymity, through which information began to flow with surprising rapidity. The pawnbroker, Berthier, had taken the precaution of asking Mateer a few seemingly casual questions as they did business in order to protect himself and in this way had deduced or guessed the name of the hotel where the man was staying. It was not, as Gautier had supposed, in the district around the Gare de Lyon, but in a small street just off Rue du Caire, an area frequented by street walkers, for whom it was conveniently placed between les Halles, with its army of market porters, and the Gare du Nord and the Gare de l'Est. There they might welcome provincial visitors eager to sample the naughty pleasures for which the capital was famous.

The owner of the hotel was able to tell Gautier and Surat that Mateer had taken a room there ten days before Lady Dorothy's murder. He had told the hotel proprietor that he had come to Paris from Marseille in order to get his hands on some money, real money, for the pickings from small-time crime in the south were not enough for a man of his tastes. He had talked freely both in the hotel and in the cafés in the quartier, boasting of his achievements and his strength and his lack of scruples. The boasting, it struck Gautier, had been a form of advertising, of letting it be known that he was in Paris and available for any illegal enterprise that would pay well. And the advertising had been effective, for everyone who had met Mateer had agreed that he was clever and ruthless and more than handy with a knife.

The advertising also appeared to have produced results, for not long afterwards Mateer was spending almost as freely as he had been talking. The cafés in St. Denis took some of his money and so did the girls. One girl in particular, a pretty little half-caste from Macao, had taken his fancy and spent a good deal of time, by day as well as by night, in the hotel with him. There had even been talk of his moving in to live with her in an apartment he would rent.

In spite of his bragging and his womanizing, Mateer did not seem to have made enemies and he had clearly not been a quarrelsome or aggressive character. So when he had been found with his throat cut everyone had been surprised, not upset for he was from Marseille, not a Parisian, but surprised.

When they had learnt as much as they were likely to, mostly from the half-caste girl, Gautier and Surat went into a brasserie and ordered bocks.

'Do you think Mateer killed the Englishwoman at the Hotel Cheltenham?' Surat asked.

'Almost certainly. How else would he have got his hands on her jewellery?'

'What should I do? Tell the director-general what we have discovered?'

'Not yet. When was this man Mateer murdered?'

'Two nights ago.'

'Good. Then his body will still be in the mortuary. Go to the Hotel Cheltenham now and find the two maids who said they saw a waiter on the morning of the murder whom they did not recognize as one of the hotel staff. Take them to the mortuary to see if they can identify Mateer as the man they saw. If they can, set some men to searching the corridors around the hotel kitchens and everywhere near the back entrance.'

Gautier reasoned that if Mateer, dressed as a waiter, had murdered Lady Dorothy, then he would have wanted to get rid of his waiter's apron as soon as he could and would certainly not have wished to be seen leaving the hotel and walking through the streets wearing it. If the apron were found it might be possible to trace the shop where it had been bought or hired.

'Collect as much evidence as you can and then write a detailed report for Courtrand. You know how inflexible he is. If he has made up his mind that Miss Newbolt killed Lady Dorothy, he will need a good deal of convincing that she did not.'

'I understand.'

'And when you take him the report, try to suggest as tactfully as you can that it would be good for the Sûreté if it can be proved that Lady Dorothy was killed by Mateer. One could say then that it was her own fault for keeping a large sum of money and her jewels in a hotel bedroom instead of locking them up in the safe. No one could blame the police.'

Surat grinned. 'One can see, patron, that you have studied the way in which the director-general's mind works.'

A waitress brought them two more bocks and took their empty glasses away with her. The brasserie was a large and popular "Brasserie des Filles", one of more than 200 such establishments in Paris which, while they existed mainly to sell beer, offered an additional attraction in the form of waitresses whose favours were also on sale, often in rooms above the brasserie. Some of the brasseries had advertised this aspect of their trade too blatantly, by making the girls wear indecently short skirts, so much so that the prefecture of police had recently felt obliged to issue a circular to proprietors, instructing them to see that their waitresses were more modestly attired. Other brasseries exploited the girls by encouraging them to rival each other in flaunting themselves before the customers, even to the point of staging displays of pretended passion and jealousy and fighting each other.

The girl who was serving Gautier and Surat that evening was tall and broad-hipped, probably from the country and, except for her sulky prettiness, she reminded Gautier of Janine. The memory of Janine provoked other thoughts. He remembered how, on the eve of his duel with the Comte de Bouttin, he and Michelle Le Tellier had made love and wondered how long it would be before they made love again, if indeed they ever did. Since his wife had left him, he had found four women who had been willing to be his mistress, for a time at least. They had given him, each in her own way, more than mere physical pleasure: affection, companionship and admiration. He supposed that this could be the reason why casual sex no longer satisfied him as it had when he had been 18 or 20. The memory of these past affairs led him, for no very good reason, into thinking of Miss Newbolt.

'The person I feel sorry for,' he told Surat, 'is Mademoiselle Newbolt. Now at least she will be released from prison.'

'I doubt that, patron.'

'Why not?'

'Even if we can prove that Mateer must have murdered Lady Dorothy, Newbolt will have another charge to face. After all, she did steal her employer's money.'

Gautier stared at him. 'Are you saying that she took the money Lady Dorothy had in her suite?'

'Yes. When she found Lady Dorothy was dead and saw the money lying on a table in the suite, she hid it in her clothes and when she returned to her room stuffed it behind the wardrobe where we later found it.'

'How do you know this?'

'She admitted as much to the juge d'instruction. That's the reason they locked her up in St. Lazare.'

12

THE DUC DE NARBONNE lived in Faubourg St. Germain, the quadrilateral of Paris bordered by the Seine to the north, by Rue de Babylone to the south, by Esplanade des Invalides to the west and by Rue des Saints-Pères to the east, where 'Le Monde', the old aristocratic families and the rich and the well connected still lived. It was a part of the city that had largely escaped the scalpel of Haussmann when he had carved up and reconstructed Paris at the request of Napoleon III and its narrow streets and old houses still survived. One of them, an 'hôtel particulier' which dated back to the 17th century, had been the home of the ducs de Narbonne for generations. Now the present duc lived in it alone among the splendid furniture, carpets and works of art which he had been collecting for the whole of his life, for unlike most of the remaining aristocrats of France, he was not only a man of great taste but of great wealth.

From the street the fiacre in which Gautier had travelled drove through an arched entrance into a courtyard in front of the house where the door was opened to him by a footman in the green and gold livery of the ducs de Narbonne. He was a boy of not much more than 17, with legs slim enough and shapely enough to show off the green and gold knee breeches and green silk stockings of his uniform. He took Gautier's visiting card with the self-assurance of a servant who knows he is protected by his master's favouritism.

The duc received Gautier in the drawing-room, a room with panelled walls painted a pastel shade of pink and a chandelier which drew attention immediately to the magnificent painted ceiling with its angels and nymphs. He was wearing a burgundy coloured smoking jacket and sat in an armchair with a rug over his knees. Although the morning was warm, a fire was burning in the grate.

The duc looked very old and very frail but his eyes were bright and alert.

'How can I help you, Inspector?' he asked.

'By answering a few questions, Monsieur le Duc, if you would be so kind.'

'Has one of my boys been misbehaving again?'

'Your boys?'

'My footmen. They are all splendid fellows, really, and almost embarrassingly loyal, but sometimes in this corrupt city they are tempted into indiscretions.'

In the past, Gautier knew, there had been more than one complaint about the duc's footmen who, after drinking too freely in the cafés of the quartier, had offended the sensibilities of solid, working-class Parisians who believed that France's greatness had been built on virtues more masculine than the footmen were apt to demonstrate. Usually the complaints had been settled amicably enough, for the duc's generosity was wonderfully effective in soothing injured pride.

'No, Monsieur le Duc, the questions I wish to ask are about an English friend of yours.'

'Not that scoundrel Oscar Wilde?'

'No. Another friend, now also dead alas, the Earl of Tain.'

Learning that he was not to be bothered by yet another minor homosexual scandal pleased the duc. His face brightened, he threw the blanket off from his knees and sat alert, seeming suddenly ten years younger. One sensed that he had deliberately been putting on a show of age and infirmity, in the hope that the police might then be prepared to deal more leniently with any trouble which his servants may have caused. His reputation for being a wicked old scoundrel was probably well deserved.

'The Earl of Tain!' he exclaimed. 'There's a ghost from the past if you please.'

'Did you know that his sister was stabbed to death in Paris a few days ago?'

'Yes, I read about it in the papers. Really shocking! But by all accounts she was a most unsympathetic character.' The duc shook his head. 'It's years since I last saw the poor earl.'

'In 1896 was it not?'

'Was it? You say that as though the date was significant.'

'It was the year of the Flower Girl Affair.'

'Holy Mother, so it was! I had forgotten.'

Gautier sensed that the duc had not forgotten that the Earl of Tain's visit to Paris had coincided with the Flower Girl trial, but that for some reason he was feigning ignorance. He wondered gloomily whether the old man would now put on a show of failing memory or even senility. He obviously enjoyed acting.

'He stayed as a guest with Madame de Nyren,' Gautier said, deciding that the best way of thwarting any game that the duc might be planning to play was by showing him how much he already knew. 'Madame de Nyren's father was one of the accused on trial.'

'Yes,' the duc agreed reluctantly. 'The earl came over to Paris to give the poor girl comfort and support.'

'She complains that he spent most of his time here with you.'

'You have spoken with Arlette then?'

'Yes, I have.'

The duc sighed. Old age had left him with few pleasures apart from that of admiring good-looking young men. Now this wretched police inspector was depriving him of his other favourite pastime—playacting. 'It was that girl in the case,' he said.

'The one they called Rosebud?'

'God in Heaven! How much more do you know? Yes, Rosebud. The earl was bowled over by her the first time he saw her in court. I cannot imagine why. A very ordinary little creature from a humble home with no looks, no fire, nothing.'

As he watched the trial, the duc told Gautier, the Earl of Tain had been more and more drawn to Rosebud until she had become an obsession and after the trial ended he was determined that he must meet her. Since he did not have the slightest idea of how this could be managed, he approached the Duc de Narbonne whom he had met years before in London. The duc had not liked the idea and had warned the earl of the risks he would be running. He might easily end up in court himself on a charge of corrupting a minor. But by then the earl was besotted with the girl and finally the duc had given in to his pleading and the meeting had been arranged.

'How did you arrange it?' Gautier asked.

'I forget exactly,' the duc replied evenly. 'I seem to recall that one of my servants managed it. These people can fix anything, you know. They can buy anything, sell anything. They can get you a girl, any girl you fancy, or a boy if you prefer it. Anyway, the earl and Rosebud did meet.'

'And what happened?'

'Evidently she was attracted to him just as strongly. They met again and then again and then every day. They could hardly bear to be separated but the earl maintained their passion was not physical and I believe him.'

'And so?'

'Finally the earl went home. He had been getting telegraph messages every other day from his wife and sister ordering him back. They were furious!'

'Did anyone else know about his infatuation?'

'No. We took every precaution to keep the meetings secret. Arlette de Nyren would have been enraged if she knew, for she had doted on the earl ever since their youthful romance.' The duc paused, frowning as he thought back to the events of a decade ago. 'And yet ironically I believe that in Rosebud the earl was recapturing the emotions of that past romance. Arlette had changed. She was no longer beautiful and her face had coarsened and lost its delicacy after her many love affairs. It must have come as a shock to the earl when he arrived in Paris and saw her. Somehow Rosebud became for him the embodiment of what Arlette had been at eighteen, young and fresh and passionately romantic; and so French of course. He had always been in love with France.'

Thinking of the past seemed suddenly to make the duc remember that he had another pleasure in life which, in spite of his doctor's advice, was still not denied him. Getting up from the armchair, he crossed the room and took a cigar from a silver box which stood on a table by the window. Hampered by rheumatism, he moved slowly and with difficulty. Watching him, Gautier could not help smiling as he recalled a widely quoted remark that had been made only recently by another old and distinguished French aristocrat when he had complained that, while in his youth he had boasted four supple limbs and one stiff one, now the reverse was true.

'Do you know if the earl gave the girl any money?' he asked the duc.

'I imagine not. As I have told you it was a platonic relationship. Besides, the poor fellow had no money to speak of. I even had to pay the man who arranged the meetings with Rosebud because the earl could not afford to.'

'The countess has money I believe.'

'If she has then she never let her husband see any of it.'

'Do you know what happened to the girl Rosebud? I heard that she married.'

'My dear man, I haven't the slightest idea!'

Gautier could see that the duc's ignorance was not dissembled. He had no interest in Rosebud, but it was not because she came from a humble background. Waiters and postmen and delivery boys from shops attracted him and he found their company more stimulating than that of the many young gentlemen in Paris who shared his perversion. Rosebud's only fault was that she was a girl.

Gautier also decided that the duc had nothing more of any value to tell him and he was about to make his excuses and leave when the footman who had admitted him to the house came into the room. He was carrying a petit blue which had just been delivered and which he handed to the duc on a silver salver. When the duc read the message, he gave a gasp and his face twisted into a grimace, as though he were in pain.

'Not bad news, I hope, Monsieur,' Gautier said.

'Most upsetting! I really am shocked! Shocked!'

'A bereavement?'

'Not exactly. It is just that a man I once knew well, a friend, a very talented and cultured man a good deal younger than I am, has been found dead in most distressing circumstances.'

'Would I know him?'

'Possibly. At one time he had a reputation in Paris. He was the poet Jean-Jacques Touraine.'

The policeman from the local commissariat who was stationed outside the entrance to Touraine's apartment had met Gautier in the past and recognized him, but like the warders at St. Lazare prison, he could not have heard of his suspension from duty. They chatted amiably.

'Who is in charge of the investigation?' Gautier asked.

'Inspector Bertot.'

'Is he upstairs?'

'No. He returned to Sûreté headquarters after the body had been taken to the mortuary. He said he would be returning later.'

'Is there no one in the apartment?'

'Only the old lady and she is suffering from a crisis of nerves.'

Gautier had forgotten that Touraine's mother had come to stay with him in Paris. 'Perhaps I should go upstairs to make sure she is all right.'

'It would be a kindness, Inspector, I am sure.'

Madame Touraine was sitting stiffly upright in a hard-backed chair, her hands folded in her lap. She wore a plain black silk dress and a black hat lay on the table by her side with three long hat pins beside it. From the way in which Touraine had spoken of his mother, Gautier had expected that she would be an anxious, retiring woman, easily alarmed. Instead she appeared determined and imperturbable. Any nervous or emotional crisis which she may have suffered as a result of her son's death had evidently abated or was being kept under control. When Gautier introduced himself she did no more than nod. He began to question her gently and tactfully about Touraine's death.

She told him that she had found her son lying dead in the bathroom of the apartment when she had risen that morning. They had dined early the previous night, eating a meal which she had prepared for him, for the woman who came in to cook for him was ill. Afterwards he had gone out and had not returned by the time she went to bed.

'Do you know the cause of death?' Gautier asked her.

'The police have suggested that it was natural, the cumulative effect of the drugs he has been taking for so many years.' She looked at Gautier defiantly. 'You knew my son was taking drugs?'

'I had heard so, Madame.'

'He was obliged to for the sake of his health. Jean-Jacques was never a strong boy. As a child he almost died more than once and it was only my care and devotion that nursed him through several illnesses.'

'Your son was devoted to you. I know that.'

'I cannot believe that his death was natural.' Madame Touraine closed her eyes for a moment and one could see that it was taking all her will power to check a burst of emotion. 'You should have seen the agony in his face, Monsieur, when I found him this morning. No, I am convinced he was poisoned.'

Gautier made no comment. The report of the medical experts would in due course give the cause of Touraine's death, although their findings might be based on probability rather than certainty. The border line between drugs and poison was a shadowy one which medical science still had difficulty in identifying.

Instead he asked Madame Touraine, 'Did you hear nothing during the night?'

'Nothing. But on my son's advice I took a sleeping draught when I retired. I sleep so badly in Paris.'

Picking up her hat, Madame Touraine began pinning it to her thick, black hair. 'Now, if you have no more questions, Monsieur, I would like to go out. I must telegraph my brother to come to Paris at once. A man is always needed on these occasions.'

'Of course, Madame. I have only one more question. Did your son tell you where he was going yesterday evening?'

'No. He simply said he had to meet a friend. But he was very excited about it. Over dinner he kept telling me that he and this friend together would be able to make a great deal of money.'

'He did not say how?'

'No. All he said was that now his money troubles would be over.'

Madame Touraine nodded at Gautier once again and left the room. She was a formidable woman and he could not help but admire the fortitude with which she was enduring the latest in a series of disappointments which must have been the milestones in her life: disappointment at having an effeminate son, at discovering his homosexual inclinations, at his notoriety, at the way in which, after brief recognition for his talent, he had drifted into obscurity. Unswervingly loyal, patriotic, honest and pious, she possessed the virtues that Gautier always expected to find in a bourgeois mother, not the excitable temperament and moody passion that foreigners associated with the French.

As soon as she had left, Gautier set to work. A combination of circumstances and good fortune had given him an opportunity he could never have expected. Had the police believed that Touraine had been poisoned, they would have searched the apartment with painstaking thoroughness, taken away any evidence which might have a bearing on his death and then left the place sealed. In any case Gautier, as he was suspended from duty, would not have been allowed inside. As it was, because Touraine's death was thought to have been from natural causes, they had done no more than question the dead man's mother and leave a policeman stationed outside the apartment. Gautier was free then to do as he wished.

He went first to the bathroom. It was a small room, only large enough to house an enamelled tin bath, a washhand stand with basin and jug, a commode and a small cabinet. The building, like most of the apartment buildings in Paris, was not equipped with running water and the only water to be had was from a tap on the ground floor. In the cabinet Gautier found a large selection of patent medicines and bottles of traditional remedies for colic, indigestion, ailing kidneys and suspect livers. In spite of Touraine's reputation as an éthéromane, there was no ether and he supposed this might be a temporary concession on the occasion of his mother's visit. Side by side with the medicaments were bottles of dye and a selection of cosmetics, including powder and rouge. The contents of the cabinet were eloquent evidence of Touraine's habits and style of living but they said nothing about his death.

The two bedrooms of the apartment presented a startling contrast. One, the guest room, was furnished with a four-poster bed with curtains, a Persian carpet, wall hangings and paintings mainly of erotic subjects. Touraine's bedroom, on the other hand, might have been the cell of an ascetic, with its iron bedstead, linoleum on the floor and bare walls. The only ornament was a beautiful medieval triptych on the mantelpiece which showed the Virgin Mary, flanked by saints. Touraine had kept his clothes in a cupboard and a chest of drawers. In the top drawer of the chest, among cravats and foulards and silk handkerchiefs, a pair of curling tongs and a box of pomade, Gautier found a pocket notebook. The first half of the book was full of random notes and jottings, ideas perhaps for articles or essays and chapter or page references to what one assumed must be books. Two lines of what might have been intended as a couplet for a poem caught his attention.

Her red lips of corruption, seeking mine,
Dripped prurient desire, unholy wine.

Gautier could not recall ever having read any of Touraine's verses and he was surprised to see what he felt must be the influence of Baudelaire in the couplet. Baudelaire, he understood, was considered outdated, somewhat 'vieux jeu', by modern French poets.

The second half of the notebook had been carefully ruled and dated to serve as an appointments diary. The entries in it, either to save space or to preserve secrecy, were brief and cryptic, consisting of no more than letters and numbers. The numbers, Gautier decided, were in all probability the times of Touraine's appointments and the letters the initials of the people he had met or the places where he had arranged to meet them. His theory was borne out by the two entries which he found against the day prior to Lady Dorothy's murder, which read:

3. SD—LDS.
7. HdL—AM.

The initials SD would stand for the Salle Delacroix where Touraine had met Lady Dorothy Strathy at three in the afternoon. It would have been at 7.00 the same evening that he called at the Hotel de Lascombes and saw André Moncade.

In the days that followed were other entries which Gautier fancied he could identify without much difficulty. Gd'E must stand for the Gare de l'Est where Touraine had gone to meet his mother when she arrived by train from Normandy. Qd'O would be Sûreté headquarters on Quai des Orfèvres, where the poet had been interviewed by IG or Inspector Gautier.

Touraine appeared to have led a busy life and against some days he had made a number of entries, at the meaning of which Gautier could only guess. FIG might well stand for the offices of the newspaper *Figaro* for which the poet was writing articles, HdV could signify the Hotel de Ville and PdC could mean the Palais des Congrès, where an exhibition of arts and crafts from the Far East was at that time being staged. Interspersed among these were other initials which, if coincidence were discounted, could well be those of the same people as Gautier himself had met or called on since his return to Paris. Thus AdN were the initials of Arlette de Nyren, DdN could stand for the Duc de Narbonne and SLP might well be the St. Lazare Prison.

Touraine, it seemed to Gautier, must have been making the same enquiries as he had been making and following very much the same trail. When he saw that the entry was followed on the same day by the initials HC, he felt a stirring of excitement. If Touraine had spoken to Miss Newbolt and she had told him of the Earl of Tain's letters, he might well have gone to the Hotel Cheltenham and, using a forged letter of authority, taken the bundle of letters from the hotel strongbox. If that were true the letters might still be in his apartment.

Putting the notebook on one side, he began searching, first in Touraine's bedroom, then in the living-room, opening drawers, looking behind cushions, pulling books from the shelves along the walls. He found no letters nor anything else of any interest.

Finally deciding reluctantly that his theory must be wrong and that he had been making too many assumptions, he picked the notebook up again. At least from that he might be able to learn where Touraine had gone on the evening before he died and the identity of the friend with whom he was going to make a fortune. The final entry in the diary was for the previous evening and the appointment had evidently been for 9 o'clock. The initials were the same as Gautier had found in an earlier entry:

HdL—AM.

13

'YOUR REQUEST PLACES me in a dilemma, Gautier,' Judge Loubet said.

'In that case I apologize, Monsieur.'

'You are asking to see the dossier of a case that was tried and settled many years ago.'

'I have my reasons.'

'No doubt. And it may be better for my peace of mind if I do not know them.'

Loubet smiled. Although he gave an impression of being solemn, reserved and on occasions pompous, he had a good sense of humour. Gautier had worked more than once on criminal cases for which Loubet had been appointed juge d'instruction and had learnt to admire and respect him. Unlike many judges, he never indulged his own prejudices and was completely fair, almost too fair some would say, in his examination of witnesses.

'My dilemma,' he continued, 'is how I am going to give you the authority to study this dossier. How can I describe your interest?'

'You might say I was a student—an unemployed student.'

This time Loubet, who knew of the circumstances leading up to Gautier's suspension, did not smile. He may have had sympathy for him. As he took a sheet of paper and began writing he said, 'I am doing what you ask, Gautier, for two reasons: because I trust your judgement and because I know you are dedicated to justice.'

Leaving the judge's rooms with the authority he needed, Gautier went to the records office of the Ministry of Justice, where the archives of criminal cases were stored. The civil servant in charge of the records grumbled at having to search for a dossier of a trial that had taken place so many years ago, but eventually he produced it and cleared a space at a table loaded with papers, where Gautier could sit down and study it.

The documents in the dossier, amounting in all to several hundred pages, fell into two main sections. Firstly, there were the papers on which the decision to take the case to court had been taken by the Chambre des Mises en Accusation; secondly, the reports of the police officers who had investigated the case and the verbatim accounts of the examinations of the accused and of several witnesses by the juge d'instruction.

The reports by officers of the Sûreté were as always concise and informative and gave an account of the events leading up to the time when the Duc de Caramond and Charles Bailly had been arrested. The suspicions of the police had first been alerted by the concierge of the building in a not very fashionable part of Paris, in which the two men had been holding their sexual orgies. The concierge had noticed three schoolgirls arriving at the building, separately but always on the same afternoon. In a fit of spite, or perhaps she had not been tipped enough, she had spoken to a friend who was engaged to a policeman working at the local commissariat. The police had made discreet enquiries and found that the apartment was owned by a cousin of Bailly. Then when they learnt that some months previously a complaint had been lodged—though never proved—against Bailly for molesting young girls, they had put a watch on the building. Three days later the trap had been sprung. Police officers forcing their way into the apartment had found the three girls naked and the duc and Bailly almost so.

From the reports, Gautier turned his attention to the accounts of the examinations carried out by the juge d'instruction. The Duc de Caramond and Bailly had at first tried to bluff their way out of trouble by claiming that they were both amateur artists and that the girls had only been posing for them in the nude. The girls had then been questioned separately, but in the presence of their parents. Simone Delon, the girl the men had called Rosebud, had been the first to be questioned and she had immediately admitted that she and her two friends had gone to the apartment where they had shared sexual experiences with the men. When asked who had arranged the secret meetings, all she had been able to say was that she had been asked to join in by her schoolfriend, Marie Desjardins.

Her reason for agreeing to go had been, she claimed, to earn money, for her parents were very poor and her mother was seriously ill. At this point her father, who had been present at the examination, had interrupted to confirm what she had said and had told the judge that his wife was now in a hospital for incurables suffering with consumption.

The juge d'instruction had then asked Simone how many men had taken part in the orgies and she had replied that on most afternoons there had been three, although she was unable to give the names of any of them. As well as choosing the names of flowers for the girls, the men had apparently decided that they themselves would each be known by the name of an animal. Bailly was to be called 'Camel', the duc 'Hippo' and the third man 'Panther'.

The two remaining girls, Marie and Noelle, had then been examined in turn. Marie, evidently the ringleader in the escapade, had admitted that she had persuaded her two friends to go to the apartment with her, but when she was asked who had first approached her and suggested the meetings, she had answered evasively, saying it was a man she knew only slightly, whose name she could not remember. Nor could she recall where and in what circumstances she had met him. Noelle had given much the same answers to the judge's questions and reading the accounts of the examinations, Gautier could only conclude that the two girls had agreed what they would say and possibly even rehearsed answers to questions which they knew would be put to them. Both of them had insisted that only the two men known as Hippo and Camel had been at the orgies and that they knew nothing of any third man.

Working his way through the dossier of the case, Gautier read the reports of the examinations of other witnesses: the policemen who had made the arrests, the concierge of the apartment building and the parents of the three girls. None of the reports added appreciably to the knowledge of the affair that he had already amassed. The concierge swore that she knew nothing of any go-between who might have brought the men and the girls together, nor was she able to say whether there had been a third man, only identifying the duc and Bailly in court as two men she had often seen entering the building.

The girls had then been examined a second time and the answers they gave to questions were very much the same, with one notable exception. Simone Delon now denied that there had been a third man. When questioned on this point by the juge d'instruction, she stuck to her second story, telling the judge that she had been confused and frightened at her first appearance before him and could not even recall ever having said that there had been a third man. When the judge pressed her she blustered at first and then began to weep until her father intervened, protesting that the judge had no right to bully the girl.

Putting the reports aside, Gautier turned to the verbatim accounts of the proceedings in court. He remembered how the Rouen newspaper had criticized the prosecution for the lack of vigour with which the case against the accused had been pressed. In French courts it was in effect the Presiding Judge who conducted the trial, questioning the accused and the witnesses, and although the prosecution and defence advocates might ask questions, they had to do so through him. Reading the questions that had been asked and the closing speeches for the prosecution and defence, Gautier could not but agree with the newspaper's criticisms. One had the impression that the three judges and the advocates of both sides had felt a certain sympathy for the Duc de Caramond and Bailly and were inclined to believe that the girls were at least equally to blame for what had happened. The question of whether a third man had been involved in the afternoon meetings had not been raised in court, nor had any attempt been made to establish who had been responsible for making the first approach to Marie Desjardins and arranging the rendezvous.

After reading through the accounts of the trial, Gautier went through the other records in the dossier and found, as he had expected, a document listing the names, addresses, ages and occupations of the two accused and all the witnesses who had been called in the trial. Simone was listed as a schoolgirl living with her parents at an address in Rue Levert. Her father's occupation was given as lamplighter.

Leaving the Ministry of Justice, he found a fiacre which took him to the 20th arrondissement and set him down at the end of Rue Levert. He reasoned that if Simone had found a husband it would most likely have been a man living in the quartier and if, as Mimi had said, the man was a grocer, then the probability was that his shop would be in the quartier as well. As he set out on foot up Rue Levert, the thought struck him that had he not been suspended from duty, he could simply have sent Surat accompanied by one or perhaps two men on the tedious and time-consuming task of tracking down a grocer. Now he would have to do it himself. The idea of tramping the streets was not appealing, so he went into the first ordinary bistro he came to and ordered himself a marc. In that part of Paris the owner of a bistro would talk more freely to a customer than to a police officer and luck was with him for the owner of the bistro he had chosen was not only friendly but knew the district well. Over Gautier's second marc he told him that there was no grocer trading locally under the name of Decartier but he knew of a Jean Decartier who owned a grocer's shop only a few minutes' walk from the bistro and who traded under the name of Leclerc.

The shop, when Gautier found it, was an unpretentious establishment, but as it was situated away from any competing shops, one might assume that it was busy and profitable, though not busy enough to justify a staff of many assistants, and when Gautier went inside he found only one man and a boy serving customers. The man was small, nondescript and older than one would have expected the husband of a girl who must still be in her mid-twenties to be. The apron which he wore was white and without stains and so was his shirt and stiff collar. His clothes and his small, neat moustaches suggested that he was a man who valued respectability at least as much as he valued money.

Gautier waited until he had finished serving and there were no customers waiting in the shop. Then he said, 'I wonder, Monsieur, if it would be possible for me to speak with your wife?'

Decartier frowned. 'My wife?'

'Yes. I am from the Sûreté and I believe she may be able to assist me in enquiries which I am making.'

'There must have been some mistake, Monsieur. My wife cannot possibly help you.'

'Why not?'

'Simone died more than two years ago.'

'I am desolate to know it, Monsieur. And I apologize if my visit has brought back sad memories.'

'It was consumption that took her from me. Simone had always had a weak chest and consumption killed her mother as well.' Decartier looked at Gautier thoughtfully and then he asked, 'Are your enquiries connected with the Flower Girl Affair?'

'Why do you suppose they might be?'

'As you are from the Sûreté, you surely know that my wife was one of the little girls in the affair.'

'Yes, I did know that.'

'People, my relatives and friends told me I should not have married a girl whose good name had been destroyed.'

'That was very harsh, surely?'

'Let me tell you, Monsieur, I have never regretted marrying my wife. And why should I have? She was a child, an innocent who had been shamefully misused. Is it not the duty of a Christian to forgive?'

Gautier sensed that this was a speech which the grocer had made many times before, a defence not so much of his wife as of his own motives in marrying her. At one time there would have been defiance and indignation in the words. Now he repeated them mechanically, almost apologetically.

'And Simone proved my judgement was right. She was a good wife who gave me everything except children and I had already two of those from my previous marriage. And it was mostly with her money that we bought this shop.'

'What were you doing before you married?' Gautier asked.

'I worked in the shop as an assistant. But the patron, Monsieur Leclerc, wished to sell. He was an old man and his two sons were both dead, one in the war and the other from cholera in Algeria. So I bought it from him.'

'Your wife had money then?'

'She came with a good dowry; very good for a girl from an ordinary family.'

Any girl whose name had been tainted with the scandal of a public trial which centred around vice, would need a handsome dowry, Gautier knew, to find a husband. And yet he remembered that Simone's reason for agreeing to take part in the sex games with the duc and Bailly had been the poverty of her parents.

'As well as helping me in the shop, my wife managed our house so well that we never wanted for anything. That was why when consumption struck her down I was able at least to send her to die in the comfort of a sanatorium in the mountains as her mother had. She had a small allowance every month which helped, of course.'

'From her parents?'

'No. It came from an uncle who had settled in England. The allowance was paid every month without fail.'

'How did the money reach your wife?'

'A messenger would bring it. One supposes that he was sent by a bank.'

'You speak as though this were in the past,' Gautier remarked. 'Does this mean you no longer receive the money?'

'No. The payments stopped as soon as my wife died,' Decartier replied and one sensed that he felt life had treated him badly, taking from him at the same time not only a hard-working wife but a useful source of income. 'Do you know I have often wondered about that. How did this uncle learn that Simone was dead? I could not write and tell him for we did not know where he lived.'

14

THE STREET IN which Gautier lived was badly lit and he did not notice the woman standing outside the apartment building until he was almost at the entrance. She stood with her back towards the nearest gas streetlamp, her face in shadow, and because she was wearing a hat he thought she must be a street walker. Respectable women did not wear hats when out at night. Then, noticing the valise which stood on the ground beside her, he looked more closely and recognized Miss Newbolt.

She looked up at him, defiantly it seemed, and said, 'I'm sorry but you were the only person I could think of who might be willing to help me.'

'How long have you been waiting here?' Gautier asked.

'I'm not sure. More than an hour anyway.'

'Then come up to my apartment. We cannot talk here.'

'So they have released you from prison,' he remarked as they walked up the four flights of stairs to his apartment.

'Yes, and I suspect I have you to thank for that.'

'It was mostly by chance that we found out who killed Lady Dorothy. I played a very small part.'

Her valise which he was carrying was small and light, too small, one would have thought, for a voyage of some weeks through Europe, but then a lady's companion would not be expected to appear in different outfits very often. Gautier could picture Lady Dorothy's luggage being loaded on to a train by porters—several suitcases, hatboxes and no doubt a wardrobe trunk.

When they were in his apartment, Miss Newbolt sat on the edge of an armchair, tense and uneasy, reminding Gautier of a woman sitting in a doctor's consulting room. He would have liked to ask her to take off her hat, but was afraid she might misconstrue the suggestion.

'How can I be of service to you, Mademoiselle?' he asked her.

'I have been abandoned in Paris,' she replied. 'That may sound melodramatic but it is the truth. The lawyer representing Lady Dorothy's family has returned to England and I have been left to make my own way home. The Hotel Cheltenham will not give me a room, even supposing I could afford to pay its prices.'

'What are your plans?'

'Tomorrow I shall telegraph my parents for money to pay my fare back to England. In the meantime I have only a few francs. I wonder, Monsieur, if you know of a small hotel or pension which would trust me until the money arrives from home.'

'Why not stay here?' Even as he made the offer, Gautier questioned its wisdom, recognizing the impulse behind it as one which had brought him trouble more than once in the past. 'As you can see my apartment is not luxurious, but I do have a guest bedroom.'

'Thank you, but I could not possibly inconvenience your family.'

'I have no family. I live here alone.'

Miss Newbolt blushed, so unexpectedly that Gautier wanted to laugh. She said, 'In that case, what would your neighbours think if I were to spend the night here unchaperoned?'

'Nothing.' He smiled as he replied. 'Perhaps we French are more understanding than the English.'

'I have no doubt that you are.'

When he took her into the second bedroom of the apartment, Gautier felt self-conscious, aware of its simplicity and lack of comfort and thinking how poor it must seem in contrast with the rooms of Lady Dorothy's London town house and even, perhaps, with the bedroom in the country vicarage where Miss Newbolt would have spent her childhood. The feeling irritated him, for he had always told himself that he would never be ashamed of his upbringing or his way of life.

'What a charming little room!' Miss Newbolt exclaimed as they went in. 'It reminds me of my own bedroom at home, except that it is cosier.'

He left her alone to unpack her valise and when she came back into the living-room she had taken off her hat and coat. Her hair was drawn back from her face and tied in a bun at the back of her head, which was not a style that suited her, making her face with its high cheekbones seem severe and almost gaunt. Gautier wondered whether she had lost weight in prison.

'May I get you something to eat?' he offered.

'Thank you, no. I am not hungry.'

'Some wine or cognac then. It may help you sleep.'

'I would enjoy a glass of brandy.'

As they sat facing each other, drinking the cognac, he asked her: 'Tell me, why did you take Lady Dorothy's money?'

'You know about that?' Miss Newbolt laughed, a laugh so hard and bright, it might have been enamelled. 'Really I took it on impulse, thinking that no one would ever know, that people would suppose it had been stolen by the person who had stabbed Lady Dorothy.'

'We would certainly have thought that if the money had not been found in your room.'

'Do you blame me? Was I not entitled to some compensation for the way she had treated me? I worked out that at the salary she was paying me, it would have taken me more than thirty years to earn that amount of money.'

'I can understand your feelings,' Gautier commented and meaning it. 'But you may even now end up in prison because of that impulsive action.'

'No, the authorities have said they will not prosecute me.'

'They must be feeling guilty for putting you in prison at all.'

'Why do you suppose Lady Dorothy brought so much money with her?' Miss Newbolt asked. 'Several thousand francs.'

'She and the Countess of Tain thought the earl was being blackmailed and hoped they could buy the blackmailer's silence, at least until the earl's daughter was safely married.'

'Why should he have been blackmailed?'

'For some homosexual indiscretion when he last came to Paris, or so they thought.'

'What evil minds they have! And the irony is that now it appears his obsession was for a young girl.'

'Can you think of any reason why anyone should wish to steal the letters he wrote to her?'

'No, why do you ask?'

'Someone has taken them from your strongbox at the hotel.'

Gautier told her how, after speaking to her in prison, he had gone to the Hotel Cheltenham and learnt that her safe deposit box had been opened on the authority of the Prefect of Police and the earl's bundle of letters taken away.

'Did you read the letters by any chance?'

'Certainly not! I would never read another person's letters. What an idea!'

Gautier's question evidently offended Miss Newbolt and her annoyance was reflected in a stiffening of not only her attitude to him but of her posture. She sat erect on her chair, her shoulders held back, her hands clasped in her lap. At any other time this reaction would have irritated Gautier as prim, bordering on hypocritical and typically English, but he knew what a harrowing experience she must have endured over the past few days. Now the strain was beginning to tell, seeping through cracks in her composure, showing in the taut pallor of her face, in her voice and in her laugh.

When she had finished her cognac and got up to go to bed, he accompanied her to the door of her guest bedroom.

'Take courage, Mademoiselle,' he said gently. 'Your nightmare is almost over. Tomorrow, if you will permit me, I shall advance you the money for your journey home and we will go together to buy the train and steamship tickets. If all goes well, you will be at home with your family by the following day.'

He bent over her hand to kiss it and when he looked up he saw tears in her eyes. She cried soundlessly, only her shoulders shuddering with each sob. Putting his hands on her face, he smoothed the tears from her cheeks with his thumbs.

'You are so good to me,' she said between sobs, 'and I don't deserve it.'

'Nonsense!'

'It is true! I have told you falsehoods. I have not been honest.'

Gautier smiled. 'In your situation I would have done the same.'

Suddenly and quickly she leant forward and kissed him on the lips. They stared at each other, he amused and surprised, she frightened by her own audacity. Surprise faded and was replaced by a more complex and subtle emotion, curiosity tinged with temptation. Then Gautier kissed her. She stared at him as he did and then closing her eyes, she reached out and pulled him clumsily to her. At first her body was tense and stiff against his, then he felt it relax and she gave a long, shuddering sigh.

Picking her up he carried her, her arms still around his neck, his mouth against hers, into the bedroom and laid her on the bed. When he began undressing her, she lay very still and he could sense her fighting an instinct to resist and push his hands away. When he touched her naked breast she gasped. Her breasts were fuller than he had imagined and firm. In not too many years her body would begin to sag and folds of skin would appear around the neck and the belly and the buttocks, but now it was still the body of a girl.

When they lay naked side by side, Gautier, guessing that she was still a virgin, hesitated. He asked her, 'Are you sure you want this?'

'Yes,' she whispered in a small, brave voice. 'Yes. Yes please.'

She lay in the crook of his arm, her head against his shoulder. Gautier had loosened her hair and a coil of it had fallen across one of her shoulders and between her breasts, looking in the darkness like a serpent against her white skin. The image of a serpent triggered off thoughts of temptation and original sin and he wondered, though not very seriously, which of them had been the tempter and which the tempted.

'If it had not been for a bullet,' Miss Newbolt said suddenly, 'I would not be here.'

'A bullet?'

'Yes. I was engaged to be married once, to an army officer. Harry Stone. He was a lieutenant and we were to be married as soon as he was promoted. Then he was posted for duty in India and soon afterwards he was killed by a sniper in Afghanistan.'

'How dreadful! And how sad for you!'

'If we had been married I would never have worked for Lady Dorothy. I would never have come to Paris.'

'Nor been in prison.'

'Nor met you.'

Turning her head she kissed him on the cheek. When they were making love she had been timid and awkward, not responding at first to his caresses, reluctant it seemed to touch him. Now she appeared to be not relaxed, but talkative and confident, as though she were pleased with the way in which she had handled an experience of which she had been secretly afraid.

'That was not the first time I've made love you know,' she said.

To have expressed surprise would, Gautier realized, be tactless, to show no surprise would be insulting, so he took refuge in a question. 'But the first time in Paris, perhaps?'

'Heavens, yes! The only other time was at home with Harry. Poor Harry! It was the night before he sailed for India. He pleaded and I had not the heart to refuse him.'

'That is easy to understand.'

Although he well understood Miss Newbolt's reasons for yielding to the entreaties of her soldier lover, Gautier had little sympathy for the sentiments behind them. A single act of love, stolen furtively and guiltily no doubt, would not be a memory to give any pleasure during their long separation. Self-denial, on the other hand, might well have sharpened their longing.

'Would you have made love to me tonight if I had not wept?' she asked suddenly.

'What a strange question!'

'I believe you acted only through pity.'

'That isn't true. You should not underrate yourself, Mary. You are an attractive woman.'

'I don't deserve your pity,' she went on, ignoring his reply. 'As I said, I have told you so many falsehoods. Why, I even lied to you tonight.'

'When was that?'

'When I told you I had not read the Earl of Tain's letters to that girl Rosebud. I did read them; all of them. There did not seem to be any harm in doing so since he was dead, and curiosity was too strong for me to resist.'

'The girl is dead too.'

'She's dead! How do you know?'

Gautier told Miss Newbolt of his meeting with Monsieur Decartier, the grocer, and explained that the Earl of Tain had been sending money secretly to Simone, his wife, through the Hotel de Lascombes ever since they had met in Paris years before. He also told her of the circumstances under which the earl had met the girl and the part she played in the Flower Girl Affair.

'Since you have been making all these enquiries,' Miss Newbolt remarked when he had finished, 'you evidently must believe that Lady Dorothy's murder was in some way connected with the earl's infatuation with Rosebud.'

'Without doubt it was.'

'And with the letters as well?'

'What interests me about the letters is why somebody should consider them important enough to have stolen them from you.'

'From what I read they appeared innocent enough to me.'

'What kind of things had he written about?'

'The letters were very sentimental and full of nostalgia, complaining how much he loved and missed her and how, if things had been different, they might have shared a life together.'

'Did he mention money at all?'

'I don't think so.'

'Or her dowry?'

'No, I am certain he did not.' Miss Newbolt paused and then added, 'This isn't helping you very much is it?'

'That isn't your fault. As he had not intended to send the letters to Rosebud, I suppose he would not have written anything of great practical importance in them.'

'What were you hoping you might have found in them?'

'I am not altogether certain. Something about the Flower Girl Affair which never came out at the trial, perhaps.'

'I'm sorry. I remember nothing like that.'

'You are tired. Perhaps tomorrow when you think about the letters you may recall something. But please don't try now. You have had an exhausting day. Why not go to sleep?'

Turning her head she looked at him and said solemnly, 'I believe I am too excited to sleep.'

'Excited?'

She had used the French adjective "aiguillonnée", a word which many might think had connotations of sexual desire and which one would not have expected an unmarried English lady to know. Gautier wondered whether Miss Newbolt's reading might have ventured further than the classical authors and poets of France and whether she might not be familiar with the novels of Rachilde and Colette, which were then very much in vogue, although many people considered them as verging on pornographic.

He touched her cheek gently with his fingers. 'Is there anything I can do,' he teased her, 'to calm you?'

'You know there is.'

He carried her breakfast on a tray into the bedroom. She was lying with her body curled up, her head on her forearms in a position which reminded him of a sleeping cat. As he glanced at her, he wondered whether he had been right in giving way to temptation and making love to her. His desire may, as she had suggested, have been triggered off by pity for her or he may, without thinking, simply have taken advantage of her vulnerability.

Whatever his motives, in the space of a few minutes he had created a new situation, as yet undefined, a new relationship between this strange and in some ways difficult Englishwoman and himself, a relationship which would depend on how each of them had been affected by the lovemaking they had shared and on what each of them would expect from the other in the future. In the next few hours they would explore each other's feelings, cautiously, even defensively, and Gautier was uneasy about the outcome. Miss Newbolt, he suspected, might expect more from him than he had the capacity to give.

Presently she awoke and looked up at him, recognizing him at once and smiling, so that he guessed she might have been dreaming of him in the few seconds of half sleep before her eyes opened. Her "good morning" was bright and unaffected, a greeting she might well have given at home to her father or a brother, if either had come into her bedroom. Sitting up in bed to take the tray, she pulled up the sheet to hide her nakedness.

While she was sipping her coffee, she said, 'I have been thinking about those letters which the Earl of Tain gave me to bring here.'

'What about them?'

'In one of them he said something which struck me as rather strange, particularly as he did not intend to post the letters. It was out of keeping with the rest of the letters.'

'What was it?'

'I cannot recall his exact words, but he seemed to be saying that he hoped the burden of conscience which had so troubled her had eased with the passage of time. Yes, "burden of conscience" was the expression he used. I am sure of that.'

'Her conscience at having agreed to take part in the orgies, I suppose.'

'I don't believe so. The earl also said something about perjury and that he was sure she had been right to be guided by her parents. She must not reproach herself for what she had done.'

'Was there nothing else?' Gautier asked.

'There was one other phrase which I do remember. "A panther may have escaped the hunters," the earl wrote, "but at least no one else suffered as a result of what you did." Have you any idea what he may have been talking about?'

'I think so.'

'And will it help?'

'As to that, I am not certain yet.'

He watched Miss Newbolt as she ate her breakfast. She held her cup of coffee delicately, as though it were made of fine, expensive porcelain, which it was not, and he remembered how Suzanne, not long before she had left him, had drunk her breakfast coffee, cradling the cup in both hands. The distinction was not a reflection of social caste or upbringing, for Suzanne's parents had been as good as anyone's, but of a mental attitude. Although she had not been more than a year or two older than Mary Newbolt, Suzanne, it had seemed to Gautier by her mannerisms, had been much more ready to accept impending middle age.

'But you know now who killed Lady Dorothy, don't you?' Miss Newbolt said.

'Yes, but we do not know why.'

'What will you do then?'

'After you have finished your breakfast you and I will make a plan.'

15

THAT MORNING, GAUTIER saw a facet of François Godilot's character of which he had previously unaware. He knew that the man was clever, skilful and resourceful in debate and, as a minister, demanding, always expecting hard work and efficiency from his staff. Now Godilot showed that he also had charm.

'Mademoiselle,' he said, after kissing Miss Newbolt's hand, 'how can I possibly convey to you my shame at the way in which you have been treated? How can I apologize and make amends?'

'Thank you,' Miss Newbolt replied, 'but really I have only myself to blame. If I had not taken the money. . . .' She smiled as well.

'We in France always take pride in our gallantry,' the minister went on, 'and it is to our undying shame that a woman so young and beautiful as yourself should have had the humiliation of being arrested and kept in prison.'

To describe Mary Newbolt as beautiful was, in Gautier's opinion, carrying chivalry to unnecessary lengths, even though that morning he thought he detected a new confidence and self-assurance in her manner which made her seem more attractive. Perhaps the moth had emerged from its chrysalis to reveal colours that were, if not dazzling, then brighter than the grey to which he had grown accustomed. And Godilot had received her and Gautier readily that morning when they had arrived at his office without an appointment, so perhaps his regret at the treatment she had been given was genuine even if his gallantry was exaggerated.

'I am glad you brought Miss Newbolt to see me, Gautier,' he continued, 'for it gives me an opportunity to demonstrate our government's regret in a tangible way.'

'What have you in mind, Monsieur le Ministre?'

'I have arranged that the Hotel Meurice will put a suite at her disposal.' Godilot smiled at Miss Newbolt. 'We hope, Mademoiselle, that you will stay on in Paris for a few days as our guest. In that way, perhaps, the memory of the inconvenience you have suffered will be erased. I chose the Meurice as you may prefer not to return to the Hotel Cheltenham after your painful experience there.'

'That is most kind of you, Minister, and I appreciate your sensitivity.'

'Does your presence here, Gautier, mean that you played a part in securing Miss Newbolt's release from prison?'

Gautier resisted the temptation to smile at the question. Godilot, he was certain, had immediately assumed that Gautier had, in spite of his suspension, continued to interfere in the investigation of Lady Dorothy's murder. At any other time he would have accused him angrily of disobeying instructions and defying him, but a display of authoritarian temper would have been incompatible with the charm he was anxious to deploy for Miss Newbolt.

'No, Monsieur le Ministre,' he replied solemnly. 'As you know, I was suspended from duty. Miss Newbolt came to see me as a friend and asked my advice.'

'What help does she need?'

'A strongbox which she was using at her hotel was opened by the police and some of her possessions taken. I told her I was sure that you would arrange for them to be returned.'

'What were these possessions?'

'A bundle of letters.'

'They were entrusted to me by a friend who is now dead,' Miss Newbolt told the minister, 'and I am most anxious to get them back.'

'Of course, Mademoiselle, I can understand that. You say that the letters were taken from your safe deposit?'

Miss Newbolt told him how she had put the letters, together with her jewellery, in a safe deposit box at the Hotel Cheltenham and of how, after she had been released from prison, when she went to reclaim her possessions the jewellery was there but the letters were missing. The management of the hotel, she added, had told her that they had allowed the police to open the box but no one else. She did not mention that Gautier, with her approval, had previously checked the contents of the box.

When she had finished Godilot asked her, 'Did the hotel management say why they had allowed the police to examine your box?'

'Because the man who came to the hotel asking for it had a letter of authority, explaining that I was the subject of an investigation and that criminal prosecution was likely.'

'By whom was this authority issued?'

'The Prefect of Police signed it, I understand.'

'I see.' Godilot looked thoughtful. 'No doubt the Sûreté thought the letters might have some connection with the murder of your employer.'

'But Monsieur,' Gautier interposed, 'how would the police have known of the existence of the letters? They had been entrusted to Miss Newbolt secretly by the Earl of Tain. Even his sister, Lady Dorothy, did not know of them.'

The question quite plainly annoyed the minister. One sensed that he was about to make a sharp retort, but then he changed his mind and only shrugged his shoulders. 'Who knows? Perhaps they did not go to the hotel looking for letters but for anything else Miss Newbolt may have concealed.' Reading the remark as an oblique reference to the money she had stolen after the murder, Miss Newbolt flushed. Godilot went on smoothly, 'At all events, Mademoiselle, you have my assurance that I'll do whatever is necessary to find those letters. They will be returned to you before you leave for England.'

'You are very kind, Monsieur.'

As they had arranged beforehand, Miss Newbolt and Gautier rose to leave as soon as they had told the minister that the authority to open her safe deposit had been signed by the Prefect of Police. But, as Gautier had anticipated, Godilot's curiosity had been aroused.

'I would like to have a few words with you alone, Gautier,' he said and then, turning to Miss Newbolt he kissed her hand once more and smiled. 'We have a police matter to discuss, Mademoiselle. I shall not detain the inspector long.' Miss Newbolt left the room and then he asked Gautier, 'Tell me, what do you know of these letters?'

'Very little, Monsieur. I have never seen them.'

'Surely the English mademoiselle must have told you something about them?'

'Only that they were written by Lady Dorothy's late brother, the Earl of Tain.'

'To whom?'

'A French girl, so I understand.'

'And why did she bring them with her to France?'

Gautier explained that for fear of compromising the girl, the earl had never posted them but that in his will he had left them to Miss Newbolt, hoping that she would be able to deliver them in person. Godilot did not appear particularly surprised by what most people would have thought to be eccentric behaviour, but then many Frenchmen, as Gautier knew, considered that all English people were a little mad.

'Since Miss Newbolt still had the letters, are we to assume she made no attempt to deliver them? If so, one wonders why.'

'She says the earl did not give an address to which she could take them.'

Godilot did not make any immediate comment. Instead, he got up, crossed the room and stood for a time looking out of the window. Eventually he said, 'Tell me, Gautier, do you think one can trust that young woman?'

'Why do you ask that, Monsieur?'

'She told a number of conflicting stories when she was under interrogation.'

'You may be right,' Gautier remarked and then he added, reluctantly as though he had not yet convinced himself that what he was going to say was true, 'I believe she may not have been entirely honest with us about those letters.'

'In what way?' Godilot asked quickly.

'She admitted to me that she had read them. We should not ignore the possibility that she took one or more from the bundle and has concealed them somewhere.'

Godilot thought he saw the implications of what Gautier was saying at once. 'If that is true she knows there is something in those letters which some person would wish to conceal. That can only mean she intends to use them for blackmail.'

*

From the Ministry of Justice, Miss Newbolt and Gautier crossed the Seine to the Right Bank and took a horse-drawn omnibus heading for the Gare du Nord, intending to make a reservation on the overnight train and boat to England. He was secretly relieved that Miss Newbolt had decided to return to London without delay, for two reasons. In the first place, although he did not regret the impulse that had led him to make love to her the previous night, his instinct told him that to prolong their brief liaison could only bring complications. Second and more important, his intuition suggested that the plan which he and Miss Newbolt had discussed that morning and which would require a good deal of improvisation, might in some way place her in danger.

It had been her idea that they should travel to the Gare du Nord in a horse-drawn omnibus rather than take one of the new motor omnibuses which were becoming more common in Paris. The driver set his team of horses off at a steady trot and as they climbed precariously up the stairs to the imperiale, or upper deck, she stumbled and fell back against him. He felt her body against his, lingering longer than was strictly necessary, it seemed.

'Soon the horse buses will have disappeared,' she told him when they had taken their seats, 'and then fiacres will be replaced by automobiles.'

'You are probably right.'

'Poor horses! What will become of them? I understand that several thousand are employed to pull the buses and fiacres of Paris.'

'Yes. The Paris Omnibus Company alone has more than 20,000 they tell me.'

'Will they be slaughtered, do you think, and used as food?'

'Without doubt. The chef at the Ritz has already earmarked several hundred for his next year's menus.'

Miss Newbolt looked at him, incredulously, for a moment, then she pouted. 'You are teasing me, Jean-Paul.'

Gautier laughed. Everyone knew about the myths which the English seemed only too ready to believe of the French: that they ate horsemeat, never bathed and beat their children. Even a woman as well read and cultured as Miss Newbolt, it seemed, was naive enough to accept them. He pinched her arm and winked.

'Let's forget about the horses,' he said. 'They will be with us for a long time yet. Instead we can talk about Lady Dorothy.'

'What about her?'

'How long had the two of you been in Paris before she was murdered?'

Miss Newbolt thought for a moment. 'Two days. A day and a half really, for we arrived at midday.'

'We know that during that time Lady Dorothy went to see a jeweller, she went to a bank and she met Touraine at the art exhibition. Do you know whether she had any other appointments?'

'Only one that I know of. On the evening of our first day here she made a social call.'

These were questions which, as Gautier well knew, he should have asked Miss Newbolt before. It was convenient to suppose that he would have done so had he not been suspended from duty, but the truth was that his handling of the investigation into Lady Dorothy's death during the first few hours following the discovery of her body had been careless and lacking in imagination. He wondered whether the success he had enjoyed in his work during the past year or two had made him lazy and complacent.

'I suppose you do not know who she went to see?'

'Not the name of the lady. All Lady Dorothy said was that she was an old friend of the family. But when she left the hotel to make the call, I went downstairs with her and told the concierge to order a fiacre for her and I gave him the address to which she wished to be driven. It was a house in Boulevard de Courcelles.'

16

GAUTIER KNEW THAT Madame Arlette de Nyren would be at home. At the Gare du Nord, while Miss Newbolt was buying tickets for her journey home, he had bought a copy of *Le Monde* and turned to the page which gave society news. There he found a list of those hostesses who were at home to receive callers that morning and Madame de Nyren's name was among them.

When he arrived at the apartment she was in her drawing-room with two other ladies and Gautier waited in the hallway until they left and then the maid showed him in. Madame de Nyren was receiving her callers that day not in the jewelled bamboo chair, but sitting erect on a sofa. Her dress, too, was more in keeping with the occasion, as though she had no wish to waste her splendid extravagances on the middle-aged ladies who would be her visitors. Only her coiffure was unconventional, the hair hanging down in separate strands, each one loaded with semi-precious stones. Some of the strands hung over her face, so that Gautier had an impression that he was looking at her through a curtain of beads.

'Men are not supposed to call on ladies in the morning, Monsieur Gautier,' she said with a hint of petulance.

'I know, Madame, but I was concerned in case, deprived as you are of the Comte de Bouttin, you might be suffering from neglect.'

'Neglect? Me? That is not a very flattering remark, is it? No, Monsieur, I have friends enough on these occasions; too many, I often think.'

What she had said was true. Calling at each others' houses, gossiping, leaving visiting cards was the recreation of ladies while their men were out riding in the Bois, or meeting in their clubs or, if they were unfortunate enough to need to work, in their banks or offices.

'I was disappointed to discover that you had not been frank with me the other evening.' Gautier decided not to continue the pretence that this was a social call.

'In what way?'

'You told me you had not seen Lady Dorothy Strathy for years, but I know now that she called on you on the day before her death.'

For a moment panic flared in Madame de Nyren's eyes but she recovered quickly. 'She did call on me but I refused to see her.'

The lie was plausible but too clumsily told to deceive. Gautier said firmly, 'And that is not true either, Madame.'

For a time Madame de Nyren sulked in silence, then she said reluctantly, 'All right, I did see the woman. But only because I supposed she had come to give me a last message from her brother or just so we could commiserate with each other. But do you know what she wanted? To find out whether he had been involved in any homosexual adventure during his last visit to Paris.'

'And what did you tell her?'

'That it was nonsense to imagine he had done any such thing. Mind you, I almost began to wonder about him when he spent all his time with that dreadful old man the Duc de Narbonne.'

'Come, Madame,' Gautier said. 'I am sure you know perfectly well why the earl went to see the duc.'

'I have no idea. Why should I know?'

'Because you would have been too curious not to have found out by one way or another. The duc is an old friend of your father. He would have told you that the earl was infatuated with a young girl and seeing her as often as he could.'

'What girl?'

'The one they called "Rosebud" in the Flower Girl Affair.'

The transformation in Madame de Nyren's expression was instantaneous, as though an actor in a medieval mummers' play had whisked away one mask to replace it with another. Petulance was replaced with an unhappiness which bordered on despair. She struggled to control her emotion with little success.

'Bertie was supposed to comfort and support me during that fearful ordeal of my father's trial. That was why he defied his wife and sister and came to Paris. And then he became infatuated with that plain, common, vulgar little prostitute who had caused all the scandal. Ironic, was it not?' she complained bitterly.

'Did you tell Lady Dorothy that?'

'Certainly not! Why should I give that dreadful woman the satisfaction of knowing that I had been humiliated?'

'Humiliated? You exaggerate, Madame.'

'Not at all. Have you any idea what an ordeal that trial was for me? For my father to be an object of censure and scorn in all Paris, the butt of obscene jokes and ribald cartoons in the newspapers? My husband even left Paris to escape the scandal, my friends abandoned me, my salon was deserted.'

'Then Lady Dorothy's visit must have revived painful memories,' Gautier remarked.

'It did but that was not surprising. That woman spread poison wherever she went, like a peasant spreading dung in the fields.'

Madame de Nyren looked at Gautier calculatingly, as a swordsman looks at his adversary before the duel begins, assessing the likely weak points in his defence. She had the reputation of being stupid and the stories about her that circulated in Paris society were meant to provoke ridicule. One of the best known was how she had once been so infatuated with a lion tamer that she had agreed to add lustre to his act by entering the lions' cage, dressed only in golden tights. Sadly the lions had shown no interest in her and as the lion tamer lost his soon afterwards, the affair ended in fiasco. Now, at their second meeting, Gautier decided it would be a mistake to underestimate either her shrewdness or her determination.

'What surprises me, Monsieur Gautier,' she said, 'is that you should be doing the same.'

'The same, Madame?'

'Digging up the scandal of the Flower Girl Affair. Poking around to discover poor Bertie's secret infatuation.'

'I am not interested in scandal, past or present. All that concerns me is why Lady Dorothy Strathy was murdered.'

'The Prefect of Police told me she was stabbed by some rascal from Marseille.'

'Yes, but I believe he was paid to kill her.'

'Have you stopped to consider the consequences if the Flower Girl scandal is raked up again? As you may know, my father is a very old man and seriously ill. To be reminded of the past, to be vilified and abused all over again would kill him.'

'I have no wish to harm your father, Madame. He has paid for what he did.'

'Then drop your enquiries, I beseech you! Take pity on him!'

'Where is your father now? In a clinic?'

'Of course not! I would never allow that! No, he is living with me, here in my home and getting the best of medical attention. Why do you ask?'

'I wondered whether perhaps I might talk to him.'

Madame de Nyren's beaded hair fluttered. Gautier had already noticed that she had a constant tremor, almost powerful enough to make one believe she was shaking her head, but in all probability it was no more than a nervous tic. Her reply, when it came, was not what Gautier had been expecting.

'Perhaps you should. Then perhaps you will understand that what you are doing is both unkind and pointless.'

'Thank you, Madame.'

'But don't expect him to make much sense. Poor papa! His memory has gone and his mind wanders from time to time.'

She led Gautier to another room in what he now realized was a very large apartment, spread over two floors. Inside the room a frail old man lay propped up with pillows in a large four-poster bed. When Madame de Nyren introduced them, he looked at Gautier without interest. His face was wrinkled and would have been strikingly white had the skin not been covered with small brown blemishes. One found it hard to believe that even a decade ago he would have found the energy for sexual pastimes with young girls.

'I am sorry to find you indisposed, Monsieur le Duc,' Gautier said.

The duc appeared to smile. His voice when he replied was a whisper, as dry and brittle as the rustle of dead leaves. 'My condition is painless, Monsieur. It is no more than the first stage in the eternal repose which I am ready to welcome.'

'Don't be so melodramatic, Papa,' Madame de Nyren said brightly. 'You will be up and about making a nuisance of yourself in a few days.' She made a show of smoothing the sheets on which her father's fragile, bony hands lay and then added, 'The inspector wishes to talk to you about the Earl of Tain.'

'The Earl of Tain?'

'You remember Bertie. We used to stay with his family in London and sometimes in Scotland when I was a girl.'

'England? Will the English ever win that war in South Africa, I wonder.'

'That was all over long ago.' Madame de Nyren turned and smiled at Gautier, raising her eyebrows as a reminder that she had warned him of her father's condition.

'Do you remember the earl's sister, Lady Dorothy?'

'The girl they called Dot?'

'Yes. She was his only sister; a few years older than me.'

The duc did remember Lady Dorothy. He scowled and said with an unexpected burst of malevolence, 'Nasty little bitch! I was delighted to hear she had been murdered. Somebody should have done it years ago!'

'Papa, you don't mean that!'

'Indeed I do.'

'Have you any idea who might have wished to kill her, Monsieur?' Gautier asked.

'A good many people.' The old man grinned at his daughter with what might have been spite or just mischief. 'Why, Arlette, I even recall overhearing you and Bertie discussing how you could get rid of his sister.'

'Papa! That isn't true!'

'Oh yes it is! It was when Bertie came over to Paris during my trial. Your husband had left you, you remember, after settling all that money on you, and you asked Bertie to leave his wife and come and live with you. He might have done but was too afraid of his sister.'

'You're making all this up.'

The duc ignored her protests. 'I recall your saying how wonderful it would be if Lady Dorothy were dead and Bertie agreed.'

Madame de Nyren looked nervously at Gautier, her twitch now a spasm of some proportions. 'My father is just teasing,' she said lamely. 'He always has to have his little joke.'

'Was the Earl of Tain present at your trial, Monsieur le Duc?' Since the duc had been the first to mention the Flower Girl Affair, Gautier did not hesitate to ask the question.

'Every day, but he was more interested in the girls than in what was going to happen to me.'

'Any girl in particular?'

'Yes, Rosebud. I cannot imagine why. She never appealed to me much. Skinny little thing with no bosoms to speak of.'

The Duc de Caramond's memory seemed to be a good deal sounder than his daughter had suggested. Gautier was encouraged, feeling that perhaps now, in the late autumn of his life, the duc might be ready to talk more freely about the escapade with the three schoolgirls than he had been at his trial, provided of course that Madame de Nyren did not interfere and prevent him from doing so. He was even more encouraged when chance came to his aid and a maid came into the room to tell her mistress that two ladies had arrived to call on her.

'I shall have to leave you two,' she told Gautier. 'This is, after all, my day for receiving visitors.'

'I understand, Madame. You must not allow my visit to upset your arrangements.'

'Don't stay too long.' One could see that Madame de Nyren did not like leaving him with her father. 'He tires easily.'

When they were alone Gautier asked the duc, 'In your opinion which of the three girls was the most attractive?'

'Violet was my favourite.' The duc giggled. 'She was bold, that one, and so vulgar! I've always found vulgarity in women particularly appealing.'

'And what did your friend Bailly think of the three girls?'

'Charles? He liked Violet as well, but more often than not he and Marigold would go together.'

'Poor Rosebud!' Gautier said lightly. 'Did no one care for her?'

'Oh, she was not neglected, I assure you.'

The duc grinned lasciviously and closed his eyes, as though he were savouring the memory of the afternoons he had spent with the three schoolgirls. His bedroom was heavy with a sweet, sickly smell and a spiral of blue smoke was rising slowly from a small bowl on a table in one corner. Gautier supposed that some aromatic herbs or incense, from the orient perhaps, were being burnt in the bowl to conceal the smell of sickness and decay. When the duc opened his eyes again they were remote and aloof.

'Was there another man there, then, to look after Rosebud?' Gautier asked.

'Those Prussian swines! They shot my horse dead beneath me.'

'I beg your pardon?'

'And now they are going to march through Paris; a victory march.' The duc stared at Gautier without recognition. 'It was you politicians who lost us the war, not the generals and certainly not the soldiers. Our leadership was undermined and destroyed by politics.'

'Did you know that after the trial the Earl of Tain met Rosebud?' Gautier asked, trying to recover from what he recognized was a losing position.

Ignoring the question, the duc continued talking about the war with Prussia, a rambling, unpatterned medley of reminiscences, invective and grumbling. He appeared convinced that the events of more than 30 years ago were still happening. His speech was slow and often slurred but even so Gautier could not help wondering whether his mind really was unsettled or whether he was dissembling, hoping in that way to deflect questions he did not wish to answer.

Suddenly he stopped speaking, looked at Gautier searchingly and seemed to switch his line of thought.

'Do you believe in ghosts, Monsieur?' he asked.

'I have no grounds for either believing or disbelieving.'

'There are ghosts; ghosts from the past. I know that now.' An expression of fear flitted across the duc's face. 'One came to haunt me the other day.'

'When was that?'

'Could it have been an omen, would you say? A presage of punishment to come?' Gautier said nothing, for the duc would not be interested in any reply. The old man went on, 'It frightens me in a way that bodily pain never has. Eternal punishment! I am afraid.'

The lechery which Gautier had fancied he could see on the duc's face had disappeared and he shivered. Was he suddenly aware, perhaps, that death might not be the long, tranquil rest for which he hoped, but an age of torment? He said slowly, 'It was the ghost of the girl's cousin, you see.'

'Which girl?'

'Violet. Violet's cousin came to haunt me.'

'When did he die?'

The question appeared to irritate the duc and he shook his head impatiently, but before he could reply their conversation was interrupted as Madame de Nyren came back into the room. She was out of breath and Gautier guessed that she had got rid of her visitors as soon as she had been able to and hurried back, unwilling to leave him alone with her father for too long.

'Look how pale papa is!' she exclaimed reproachfully. 'Have you been bullying him?'

'In no way, Madame. The duc has talked freely and willingly.'

'About what?' Madame de Nyren's nose poked through her screen of beads and hair, sharp with suspicion.

'The Earl of Tain, mainly, and the Flower Girl Affair.'

The duc was showing no interest in their conversation. His eyes still had a distant, dreamy expression, as though his consciousness had moved out of the present into a world that existed either in the past or only in his troubled imagination. Suddenly he began pulling at the sparse, white hair that lay neatly combed across his skull.

'Arlette,' he said plaintively, 'at what age does one appear in the next world?'

'Why, after one dies of course, Papa.'

'I don't mean that! How does a person look in appearance when he arrives in paradise or in hell? As he last looked on earth? Has he the face of an old man or does he look as he did in his prime of life?'

'I don't understand your question. In heaven we will be as spirits, not in mortal form.'

'Stupid girl!' the duc cried, almost in tears with impatience. 'If I come back to haunt you after I die, will I have white hair or any hair at all? Can a ghost be bald?'

'Now, Papa!' his daughter said sternly. 'You must forget these fantasies and rest. Otherwise you will exhaust yourself.'

Stepping forward to the bed, she removed the pillows which were propping up her father in a sitting position and helped him to lie back, smoothing the bedclothes as she did so. The duc made no protest, accepting her attentions mutely. He may, in fact, already have been exhausted. Then Madame de Nyren led Gautier from the bedroom.

'As I told you, Inspector,' she said as they were walking towards the entrance hall of the apartment, 'my father's mind wanders. You should take no account of anything he may have told you.'

'By no means everything he said was nonsense.'

'People have been very kind. He has many gifts of flowers and fruit.'

'And visitors?'

'Oh yes, scores. The Prefect of Police has called more than once.' The look which Madame de Nyren gave Gautier as she mentioned the prefect's name was not wasted on him. She went on, 'His old friend Charles Bailly also came to see papa before he left Paris to travel abroad. Then there was a servant. Some fellow who knew papa years ago but who was a stranger to me. Was that not kind of him? Oh yes, and the Comte de Bouttin called only yesterday.'

'The comte has recovered then?'

'Not fully. His hand is in a frightful state and the doctor is not sure that he will ever regain the sight of one eye completely, but he is up and about.'

'I'm pleased to know that.'

When they reached the entrance hall of the apartment, Madame de Nyren stopped and faced Gautier. 'I hope, Monsieur,' she said, 'that now you have spoken with my poor father you will decide not to pursue these enquiries you have been making into the Flower Girl Affair any further.'

'I cannot promise to do that.'

She pushed her beaded hair away from her eyes, possibly so that Gautier could see the anger which defaced what was left of the beauty in her face. She said, 'Are you forgetting, Monsieur, that I have powerful friends?'

'You are referring to the Prefect of Police, I assume.'

'You can be stopped from pestering people, by force if needs be.'

'Madame,' Gautier replied, 'as I suspect you are aware, someone has tried to do that already.'

17

THE COMTE DE BOUTTIN had made a remarkable recovery. When Gautier called on him that afternoon he was standing by the empty fireplace in his apartment, his right arm in a sling, a little pale but erect and proud. While he was still married to his American heiress, the fashionable society painter Boldini had painted a portrait of him, which had been hung in the Salon and won praise from the critics. Although some years had passed since then, he seemed scarcely to have changed and still had the same slim, youthful figure, the smooth, pink face, the cold blue eyes and haughty expression. In spite of his many debaucheries, the succession of sexual adventures and no shortage of fine wines and brandy, the comte had managed to remain astonishingly fit.

Gautier had been doubtful whether the comte would be prepared to meet him and when he was shown into the room by the comte's one servant, he said, 'I am indebted to you, Monsieur, for agreeing to see me.'

'I only did so,' the comte replied acidly, 'because I was curious to know what possible reason you might have for wishing to speak to me.'

'I will come to that presently, but first may I enquire about your injuries. I trust they are healing.'

'Well enough, well enough. When it is over I shall still have the thumb and one finger of my hand intact. Enough to lift a glass of wine or to pinch the thigh of an attractive woman. What else should a man need?'

'I am desolate to know the wound was so serious.'

'The fault was my own. I should have fought with my left hand. That would have been sufficient against you, Monsieur.'

Understanding the reason for the comte's bitterness, Gautier curbed his irritation. To have been injured, even by a mischance, in a duel with a man whom he would regard as an unworthy opponent, must have hurt the man's pride. 'I am sure you are right,' he said. 'I have no skill with the pistol.'

'You should be thankful. At least you emerged from our duel alive.'

'Yes, but without satisfaction and without honour.'

The answer seemed to meet with the comte's approval for his attitude softened perceptibly and he looked at Gautier as a man travelling in a foreign country might, surprised to find someone who spoke his language. 'I understand and respect your feelings, Monsieur. That accident with the pistol did us both an ill service.'

'Was it an accident?'

'Fortunately for those of us who use them, pistols rarely explode.'

'Has it occurred to you that somebody may have tampered with that pistol?'

'With what object? To kill or maim me?' The comte smiled. 'I have enemies, of course, but none of them would stoop to such a despicable action.'

'Perhaps I was meant to have had that pistol.'

'If you were the intended victim it would have meant that there was only one chance in two of your being injured. You were given a free choice of weapon, remember.'

'Unless both pistols had been tampered with.'

'But yours did not explode.'

Gautier realized immediately that the comte could not have been told that he had been the only one to fire a shot in the duel. In the panic of the moment his seconds may have forgotten to mention it or they may have thought that by doing so they might only add to the comte's sense of shame. He said, 'Forgive me for being candid, Monsieur, but I suspect that you were asked to provoke me into a duel. After all, you had no real grievance against me.'

The comte said nothing, so Gautier continued. 'Let us suppose that whoever asked you to do that wished me to be maimed or even killed. Then, rather than trust to the accuracy of your aim, he arranged that both pistols would explode when they were fired. In that way he would think that his plan was bound to succeed. The only reason it did not was that I never fired the pistol I chose.'

Still the comte did not speak. Instead he began to stride from one end of the room to the other, his good hand thrust behind his back, his fist clenched. Although one could sense his agitation, he managed to suppress it, a skill of self-discipline Gautier had often noticed in the aristocracy, developed no doubt by the strict discipline imposed on them by governesses and tutors during childhood. Whatever thoughts were being spawned in his mind were a long time in conception and, as he waited, Gautier glanced around the room.

The comte was living in the garçonnière which he had acquired while he was still married and furnished at his wife's expense. It had featured prominently in the divorce that followed, when it was proved that he had entertained a whole succession of ladies there, from duchesses to midinettes. During the case, newspapers had delighted in reporting how much money the comte had spent on decorating the garçonnière with Persian rugs, antique furniture, silk curtains and fine paintings. But all these had gone now, taken away by his wife. Today the apartment was drab, the carpets worn, the walls dingy. By no standards was it large enough to be a permanent home for a man of the comte's position but, as all Paris knew, he was living on the edge of poverty.

'Monsieur.' He finally stopped pacing and faced Gautier. 'You suggested that I had been asked to provoke you into fighting a duel. The truth is a good deal less honourable than that. I take no pleasure in admitting that I was paid to fight you.' He smiled bitterly. 'The Comte de Bouttin belongs to one of the oldest and noblest families of France. His ancestors have fought and died for king and country through centuries. Who would have thought that his sword would have ever been for hire?'

'May one ask who it was who paid you?'

'I have no objection to your asking, Monsieur, but frankly I do not even know the name of my paymaster.'

'How can that be?'

'It was all arranged through an intermediary. A Monsieur Fosse, whom I had never previously met, came to see me and offered me a very substantial sum of money if I engaged you in a duel.'

'Monsieur Fosse was one of your seconds in the duel, was he not?'

'Yes, that was part of the arrangement. I was to choose a friend who would act as my principal second, just for the sake of appearances, but Fosse took care of everything else.'

'Including providing the pistols?'

'Yes.' The comte looked at Gautier defensively. 'You will be wondering, no doubt, why I ever consented to such a thing. All I can say, Monsieur, is that a man has to live. After the shameful way my wife behaved, I cannot afford the luxury of pride.'

He waved one hand deprecatingly at the room around him and continued, 'Many people sympathized with my wife. Why should they? Our marriage was not a love match but a contract. I was to give her a title, a name, a place in society otherwise out of reach to a railwayman's daughter, and she was to provide the wealth to maintain that place. I more than fulfilled my part of the contract. I not only gave her a title, but I taught her about breeding and good taste. I filled her house with works of art, brought great musicians to play for us. Our carriages were drawn by thoroughbred horses, our cellars filled with great wines. I even chose her clothes. And then, when she thought she had taken all I had to offer, she discarded me.'

When the comte's indignation appeared to have spent itself, Gautier asked him, 'Now that you have reconsidered it, do you still think your injury was an accident?'

'No. I can see how it was all planned now. Somebody wished to dispose of you and did not care if I was killed as well.'

'Have you any idea who might have been responsible? For whom Fosse was working?'

'Not the slightest. But if I can find out, you can be sure he will pay for his insolence, for using me, for soiling my honour.' The comte's anger began to mount.

'I can think of a way whereby we can find out who it was.'

'How?'

'We could arrange to fight another duel.'

The comte's habitual mask of haughty boredom was shattered by astonishment. 'You cannot be serious, Monsieur!'

'Why not? You have already said you could fight me left-handed.'

'But what purpose would a second duel serve?'

'Let me explain what I have in mind.'

*

'Gautier, I cannot understand how you could have said such a thing!' the Prefect of Police exclaimed.

Gautier could not remember ever having seen the prefect so agitated. The air of scholarly detachment, the outward calm had vanished and been replaced by a nervousness which showed in his quick, staccato speech. Even his hands shook.

'Monsieur, the management of the Hotel Cheltenham assure me that the authority to search Miss Newbolt's strongbox bore your signature.'

'Then it was forged.'

'Very probably.'

When Gautier had arrived back at his apartment from his visit to the Comte de Bouttin, he had found a policeman from the local commissariat waiting for him with a message. The Prefect of Police, he was told, would be obliged if the inspector would call at his office as soon as he conveniently could.

'Why did you have to tell the Minister of Justice?'

Gautier explained that he had gone to see the minister only to complain that Miss Newbolt's bundle of letters had been taken. The fact that the authority to search the strongbox had allegedly been signed by the prefect had happened to come up in conversation. He felt it hard to understand why, as appeared to be the case, the prefect should be afraid of the Minister of Justice. In France, a firmly entrenched senior functionary had more real power than any temporary incumbent of a ministerial post.

'What were these letters anyway?' the prefect asked.

'Some that had been written by the Earl of Tain to a French girl. He was Lady Dorothy Strathy's brother. The girl was the one known as "Rosebud" in the Flower Girl Affair.'

'I see.'

Gautier told the prefect that the Earl of Tain had been writing regularly to Rosebud but had not sent the letters for fear of compromising her. 'In his will he left the letters to Miss Newbolt, asking her to bring them to Paris and deliver them to the girl.'

'But what was in the letters? Who would wish to steal them?'

'I cannot say, unless they revealed facts about the Flower Girl Affair which never emerged during the trial.'

'Did Miss Newbolt read the letters?'

'Yes. Apart from the earl she was the only person who did.'

'And did she find anything,' the prefect paused, looking for exactly the right word, 'anything incriminating in them?'

'She says not.'

'She may not have realized it even if there had been.' He paused. 'Or she may be lying.'

'I suppose that is possible,' Gautier said in the same reluctant tone as he had used when speaking to the Minister of Justice. 'If she did find something in the letters which would cause a scandal, she would not necessarily tell us. She may have taken one or more letters from the bundle and be keeping them.'

The prefect appeared to be thinking deeply. One had the impression that he was far from happy about what he had heard of Miss Newbolt and the letters. Presently he said, 'She was released from prison yesterday. Have you any idea where she spent the night?'

'She stayed in my apartment, Monsieur.'

'I see. And do you know what her plans are?'

'I believe she intended to return to England as soon as she could, but this morning the Minister of Justice invited her to stay on in Paris for a few days at the government's expense.'

The prefect paused and once again Gautier had the impression that he wished to choose his words very carefully. Finally he said slowly, 'You are too young, Gautier, are you not, to have been involved with the Flower Girl Affair?'

'Yes. I had a very junior position then.'

'Precisely. You should tell the English lady this. The Flower Girl Affair is dead and forgotten and it is perhaps better that it should remain that way. Anyone who begins to meddle in it might be putting themselves in jeopardy. I am not exaggerating when I say that their lives might even be in danger.'

The shadow of the wine bottle fell across the table, dividing it, but not equally, in two. Gautier and Surat were seated at the larger of the two segments, Duthrey at the smaller. The shadow and the pale light from the hissing gas lamp on the wall of the apartment and the smoke from Duthrey's cigar which hung idly on the air, seemed somehow to invest the room with an air of secrecy, so that the three men had the look of conspirators. Gautier found himself wanting to talk in a hushed voice.

'I cannot understand why you are doing this, old friend,' Duthrey complained. 'Another duel?'

'Yes,' Gautier replied patiently. Duthrey had already asked the same question and made the same comment three or four times. 'And at the same place, the same time of day and in identical circumstances.'

'This could put an end to any chances of your being reinstated at the Sûreté. It could mean the end of your career.'

'Possibly. On the other hand it may serve, if not to justify my agreeing to take part in the first duel, then at least to provide the authorities with a reason for leniency.'

'I hope I shall not regret consenting to be your second again.'

'I am grateful for that. And were you able to persuade your friend Marigny to come with us to the Bois?'

Gautier had called on Duthrey at the offices of *Figaro* earlier that evening and told him of his plan to stage a second duel with the Comte de Bouttin. With reluctance, Duthrey had agreed to find out whether Marigny would be willing to play the same role as he had at the first encounter.

'Yes. He will do so.'

'What about the Comte de Bouttin's seconds?' Surat asked.

'The comte himself is arranging that,' Gautier replied. 'He has no doubt at all that his friend Monsieur Raspail will be willing to act as principal second.'

'But one supposes that the mysterious Monsieur Fosse will not be there,' Duthrey observed.

'No. Fosse appears to have disappeared just as mysteriously as he appeared, that is if Fosse was ever his name.'

'What will you do?'

'We have fallen back on a little strategem. We have hired an actor to play the same part as Fosse did at the first duel. The comte was fortunate enough to find one at short notice who does not look unlike Fosse.'

'From what you have said,' Duthrey remarked, 'one can only conclude that you and the comte are stage-managing this business together.'

'We are, yes.'

'Many people would ask you what your purpose is, but I will not. I prefer not to know.'

Gautier laughed. He sensed that Duthrey, who he knew was secretly rather proud of the part he had played in the first duel, suspected that he might be made to look foolish if the second turned out to be some kind of charade or burlesque. In the hope of convincing him that the duel should be treated seriously, he began explaining the arrangements he had made about pistols. The Comte de Bouttin had agreed to provide a pair of pistols which would be brought to the Bois in a box similar to the one used for the first duel, by the actor impersonating Fosse.

'Let us hope that somebody remembers to look down the barrels before the pistols are loaded,' Duthrey said acidly.

'No pistols will be fired tomorrow, I can promise you that.'

'Then what do you hope to achieve by this duel?'

'Before I answer that, let me check on the other arrangements we have to make for tomorrow morning.' Gautier turned to Surat. 'Were you able to discover what we need to know?'

'Without difficulty, patron. The Minister of Justice is entertaining friends to dinner at his home tonight.'

Earlier that afternoon Gautier had met Surat and asked him if he could establish where three people would be spending that night. It was the kind of enquiry at which Surat was adept. He had a flair for making friends with, and winning the confidence of, ordinary people, especially family servants. By spending an hour or two in the bistros which they frequented, he could extract a wealth of information about their masters and mistresses, their movements, their habits, their virtues and their failings.

'The dinner party is seen to be important for the minister's political future,' Surat continued. 'A former president is among the guests and so is the editor of *Le Monde*.'

'So we can be reasonably sure that Monsieur Godilot will be spending the night at home.'

'I would think so. Men of such eminence are unlikely to desert their wives after dinner and go off to one of those houses with large numbers in Rue Richelieu.'

Surat was referring to the maisons closes, or brothels, of which there were over a hundred in Paris and which were a great attraction to visitors from the country and overseas. It was customary for such establishments to advertise themselves by having large, illuminated numbers above their doors. Some of the more expensive among them were known to attract a high class clientele of club men, bankers and diplomats and some were famed for the sumptuous elegance of their décor and furniture.

'Not the Minister of Justice anyway,' Duthrey remarked. 'Everyone knows that his wife keeps him firmly under her thumb.'

'What about the Prefect of Police and Madame de Nyren?' Gautier asked.

'By a coincidence the prefect is dining at the home of Madame de Nyren.'

'It's no coincidence. He spends a good deal of his time there,' Duthrey said, 'and I think I know why. Her father, the Duc de Caramond, is dying you know.'

'Why should that be a reason?'

'Haven't you noticed that when a man is dying many of his friends and acquaintances start calling to see him. In my view it isn't mere morbid curiosity. They go hoping to hear some startling scandal. Dying men are supposed to be eager to talk about their shameful past, to cleanse their consciences. And it isn't only to the priest that they talk.'

'It is unfortunate that the prefect is dining at Madame de Nyren's home tonight of all nights,' Gautier grumbled. 'He is her devoted admirer and who knows, he may well spend the night there rather than at home. We won't know.'

'Another difficulty,' Surat told him, 'is that Madame de Nyren does not have a telephone.'

The French with their inbred conservatism had been slow to accept the potentially dangerous invention from America which enabled strangers to penetrate the privacy of one's home, and although telephones were now to be found in government offices, police stations and the homes of the affluent and progressive, they were still relatively rare. The Minister of Justice and the Prefect of Police had been provided with telephones in their homes to help them in their official duties, but Madame de Nyren, as Gautier had observed on his visits there, had not so far installed one.

'This is what we will do.' Gautier knew that Surat responded well to instructions that were precise and which left no room for judgement or discretion. 'At five o'clock tomorrow morning you will go to the Hotel de Lascombes and arrest the proprietor, André Moncade. Take two men with you, not because he is likely to resist arrest but so that you will be free to do other things.'

'On what charge do I arrest him?'

'He has been stealing money which was sent every month from London for a Madame Decartier. There will be other charges later but that will do for the time being.'

'And we bring him to the Bois de Boulogne?'

'Yes and on the way you stop at the first police commissariat which you come to and make your telephone calls.'

The two telephone calls, Gautier had already told Surat, would be to the Minister of Justice and the Prefect of Police. The message Surat was to give in both cases was the same; that André Moncade had been arrested and was being taken by the police to the Bois de Boulogne, where Inspector Gautier had an appointment with the Comte de Bouttin.

'Give the message as simply and as quickly as you can and then end your call. Don't give them time to ask any questions. Tell them you are from the Sûreté, nothing more and on no account give your name.'

'And what if the prefect is not at home?'

'It will not matter. You will in any case send a police officer from the commissariat to Madame de Nyren's home with the same message, for she must get the news as well. If the prefect is not at home, we may assume he will be with her and she is bound to tell him.'

'And then we bring Moncade to the Bois?'

'Yes, to the spot which I have already described to you where the comte and I fought our duel,' Gautier said, and then he added, 'Try to time yourself to arrive just before six which is when we will be meeting the Comte de Bouttin and his seconds.'

'Marigny and I will have to call for you not later then five. That means the best part of another night's sleep lost.'

Duthrey was still complaining, but good humouredly, and Gautier wondered whether he was beginning to guess the object behind the elaborate arrangements they were planning. Although one might think from his manner that Duthrey was happy living in the straightjacket of yesterday's conventions, he had a shrewd brain and a flair for disentangling the truth from the most tightly knotted circumstances. He would have made a good detective if only he had been endowed with rather more physical courage.

'Then we must allow you to get home to your bed, old friend, but first take another glass of wine.'

'Thank you, no. I make it a rule never to drink more than one litre of wine a day since I suffered that crise de foie last winter.'

Soon afterwards, Duthrey left them and Gautier went over the arrangements for the arrest of Moncade with Surat. He also made him repeat the message he was to pass to the minister, the prefect and Madame de Nyren the following morning. When they had finished the rehearsal he put a hand on Surat's shoulder.

'I am conscious of what a risk you are taking for me and I appreciate it. If our plan misfires you could lose your position at the Sûreté.'

Surat shrugged his shoulders. 'Patron, unless I can work for you I would rather be back in an ordinary commissariat.'

They shook hands as Surat got up to go, but before they could leave the living-room they heard a knock on the door of the apartment. 'Duthrey is back,' Gautier guessed. 'I wonder what he has left behind.'

But when he opened the door he found not Duthrey outside but Miss Newbolt. She looked flushed and excited. Gautier looked behind her for her luggage but she had no valise with her.

'Don't tell me you missed the train.'

'No,' Miss Newbolt said and laughed. 'I changed my mind.'

Depression, heavy and pervasive, flowed into Gautier, bringing with it an astringent self-reproach. Miss Newbolt had postponed her return home and come to him in the hope of spending another night with him and the fault was his. Casually and thoughtlessly he had aroused in her an expectation which he had no wish to fulfil. Now he would have to tell her so and see the hurt in her face.

Surat, embarrassed by her arrival, was trying maladroitly to escape. He had been close to Gautier for long enough to have observed the women, the brief liaisons, the mistresses, and although he did not disapprove of them, may even have envied Gautier for them, to be there when his chief was with them made him acutely uneasy. When finally he managed to extricate himself, Gautier and Miss Newbolt went into the living-room.

'What made you change your mind?' he asked her.

'Two things. First, on my way to the Gare du Nord I decided to call in at the Hotel Meurice to see whether they really would have put me in a suite as the Minister of Justice had promised. Do you know he was as good as his word? They were expecting me at the hotel and showed me to the suite. Jean-Paul, I have never seen such luxury! It was far better than Lady Dorothy's rooms at the Cheltenham.'

'So you decided to stay and enjoy the luxury?' Gautier was amused and touched by her excitement.

'Yes, but only for a few hours. I had my valise with me, you see, and there was plenty of time before the boat train was due to leave. So I unpacked and had a bath. You cannot possibly imagine how enormous the bath is and it has running water. They even sent a chambermaid in to help me.' Miss Newbolt laughed with pleasure. 'If only my sisters could have seen me!'

'You said there were two things which made you change your mind,' Gautier prompted Miss Newbolt. He was still unsure of why she had called on him.

'Yes. The second was a visit from the Prefect of Police.'

'Did he come to warn you?'

'Warn me? Of what?' The question puzzled Miss Newbolt and her face screwed up in a frown which spawned a rash of wrinkles around her eyes. 'The prefect was charming. He arrived when the tea which I had ordered was being brought into the suite and he joined me for a cup. The purpose of his visit was simply to apologize for the way I had been treated.'

'The Minister of Justice had already done that.'

The minister and the prefect, it seemed to Gautier, were treating Miss Newbolt with a consideration and gallantry that were surprising. In his experience the authorities in France were slow to recognize their mistakes and even slower to admit them. If Miss Newbolt accepted their chivalry so unquestioningly then it might be because the police in England were habitually more courteous than their French counterparts.

'The prefect did more. He told me the authorities have decided to compensate me for the indignities I have suffered.'

'Does that mean he gave you money?'

'No, he offered me money; a very generous sum in my opinion. It will be brought to the Hotel Meurice first thing tomorrow morning.'

'You accepted his offer then?'

'Of course.' Miss Newbolt looked at Gautier doubtfully. 'Are you saying I was wrong to do so?'

'Not at all. And you are staying on in Paris tonight?'

'I must, if I am to get the money.'

Gautier remembered his conversation with the Prefect of Police that afternoon. The prefect had been anxious to know of Miss Newbolt's movements. He had suggested that her life might be in danger. It was too late to warn Miss Newbolt that the offer of money might have only been a ruse to keep her in Paris for one more night; too late because the boat train for England would have already left.

18

As the carriage moved into the Bois de Boulogne, the horses' hooves slicing the dawn's silence into measured staccato portions, Gautier felt a sense of déjà vu. But then he had been there before; history was repeating itself. Not only was he travelling in the same carriage with the same friends to an assignation with the same man, but once again, on account of a woman, he had not slept in his own bed.

On the eve of his first duel with the Comte de Bouttin he had spent the night in the bed of Michelle le Tellier. This time it had been different, for he had not shared the bed of Mary Newbolt in the Hotel Meurice as he had once feared he might have to, for when he took her back to the hotel she clearly did not expect him to stay there with her. He wondered whether this was because she wished to explore and enjoy the luxury of her suite alone, or whether the night she had spent in his apartment had not been as entrancing for her as his vanity had assumed.

After leaving her in her suite, he had stayed in the hotel, sitting up in a room opposite hers which the hotel had put at his disposal, sitting with the door slightly ajar and watching. Although he had not been by any means convinced that her life was in danger, he felt he had a moral obligation for her safety, since if she was in danger then it was he, not knowing that she would stay on in Paris that night, who had put her there. He had arrived back at his apartment only in time to shave and wash and change his clothes before Duthrey and Marigny had called to collect him.

The morning differed from the one when he had last driven through the Bois de Boulogne in another respect. The dawn on which he had gone to fight his duel with the Comte de Bouttin had been fine, with the first sunlight falling through the branches of the trees on to the dew. Now it was cold and wet, with the aftermath of a fine drizzle still lingering in the air and the trees had not yet shaken themselves free of the night's darkness.

The weather may have affected Gautier, for he felt a sense of gloom and with the gloom, pessimism. The plan which he had contrived the previous night now began to seem clumsy and hopelessly speculative, too dependent on good timing and on other people behaving in the way he anticipated. As they approached the rendezvous in the Bois where the first duel had been fought, his pessimism turned into dismay. His plan seemed to be misfiring, for he saw that the Comte de Bouttin had already arrived and was accompanied by his principal second, Raspail and the actor who was to impersonate Fosse. Standing with them was a woman whom he recognized as Madame de Nyren, but the four of them were alone. Surat had not arrived with Moncade and his two escorting policemen. It had been part of Gautier's plan that Surat and his prisoner should be at the rendezvous before he and the Comte arrived and he could not understand what could possibly have delayed them.

As their carriage drew to a halt, Madame de Nyren recognized him. She had been talking animatedly to the comte and now she rushed over to Gautier. Her hair was in disorder, the coat she was wearing was partly unbuttoned, her cosmetics had been applied carelessly. She must have risen and dressed in haste as soon as she received Surat's message.

'Is this true, Inspector,' she demanded, 'that you and Sébastien are going to fight a second duel?'

'As you can see we are both here, Madame, so are our seconds, so are our pistols.'

'It is folly! Madness! I forbid it!'

'If you wished to stop the duel why did you not bring your friend the Prefect of Police with you?'

For a moment Madame de Nyren looked confused. Twenty years previously she would probably have blushed. She said reluctantly, 'The prefect went home to change.'

'To change?'

'He could scarcely have come out here in his evening clothes, could he?'

Gautier could not make up his mind whether he should believe what Madame de Nyren had just told him. If the prefect's decision to spend the night at Madame de Nyren's apartment had been on an impulse, he would only have had evening clothes to put on in the morning. On the other hand it was unwise to discount the possibility that he had gone, not to change his clothes but to get help, and in that case he might well arrive with police officers from the Sûreté, ready to arrest Gautier and the comte. His anxiety sharpened. If the prefect arrived with policemen before Surat, Gautier's plan would collapse and he began to wonder how he could possibly have thought that it might succeed.

'Sébastien is in no condition to fight a duel,' Madame de Nyren persisted.

'That is a matter you should discuss with him, Madame.'

'Are you prepared to take advantage of his disability? To fight a crippled man?'

Gautier shrugged his shoulders. 'The comte believes that even despite his injuries he would be more than a match for me in a duel and he is probably right.'

Madame de Nyren turned away angrily and started walking back to where the Comte de Bouttin was standing with his seconds. As she did so, Gautier, to his immense relief, saw that Surat was arriving. He, Moncade and two policemen were crowded together in a fiacre, which the coachman was driving at a recklessly fast gallop along one of the many paths which ran through the Bois. The frenzied haste of their arrival, with Surat waving through one window of the fiacre and a policeman almost falling out of the other, was so comical that at any other time Gautier would have laughed.

When the fiacre came to a halt, Surat dragged Moncade out and thrust him roughly forward. 'Here you are, patron. Here's the scoundrel!'

For a man who had been arrested in his bed before first light, Moncade had kept his composure remarkably well, but all his sangfroid could not conceal the uneasiness in his eyes.

'Inspector Gautier!' he exclaimed. 'I should have known that you would be responsible for this circus performance.'

'It is no performance, I assure you.'

'You have no right to arrest me. You have been suspended from duty.'

Gautier nodded in the direction of Surat. 'I didn't arrest you. It was this officer.'

'As I have already told him, he will regret it.'

Surat and the two policemen he had recruited for his assignment stood watching, puzzled no doubt, and curious to know why they had been told to bring a prisoner to the Bois de Boulogne at that hour of the morning. Gautier knew that by obeying his instructions Surat had laid himself open to disciplinary action in the Sûreté and it would be better that he were not there if, as Gautier expected, the Prefect of Police and the Minister of Justice arrived. So he took him on one side.

'Take your two men,' he told him, 'and wait out of sight somewhere in the trees. I hope you will not be required again, but one never knows!' Then he turned to Moncade. 'You cannot rely on your influential friend to extricate you from this predicament.'

'What predicament?'

'The law can deal with the matter of the money you stole from Monsieur Decartier in due course.'

'The money was never intended for him.'

'Nor for you, but we can leave that to the judge to decide. First you have to give satisfaction for something else you did, a personal wrong you committed.'

'What are you talking about?'

The Comte de Bouttin was standing with his seconds and the doctor and Madame de Nyren some fifty paces away. It had been part of their plan to keep the two supposed protagonists in the duel apart. Gautier beckoned to the comte who, after shaking off Madame de Nyren's restraining arm, came over to him.

'You were responsible for this gentleman's injuries,' Gautier told Moncade. 'And he demands satisfaction.'

'I have never seen him before in my life.'

'That may well be true, but you arranged through a man named Fosse that the Comte de Bouttin should be paid a sum of money to challenge me to a duel.'

'This is absurd! I have not the remotest idea what you are talking about.'

'And on your instructions Fosse tampered with the pistols he provided for the duel, so that the comte and I would both be seriously injured, perhaps even killed.'

'I can only repeat that I know nothing of this business.'

The Comte de Bouttin reached out and grabbed Moncade by the forearm. In spite of having the whole of one side of his face bandaged and his right arm in a sling, or perhaps because of it, he looked menacing enough to frighten anyone of a timid disposition and the anger in his expression made him appear even more dangerous.

'Are you denying that you were responsible for the accident that disfigured me?' he demanded.

'Most categorically.'

'I do not believe you, Monsieur. I may yet lose the sight of my right eye. You are responsible and I demand satisfaction.'

'What satisfaction?'

'We are going to fight a duel, you and I. Here, with pistols, exactly as Monsieur Gautier and I were tricked into doing.'

'I have no intention of fighting with you.'

'You may do as you please. You will be given a pistol for your defence. Should you decide not to use it. . . .' The comte shrugged his shoulders. 'I shall use mine, you can be sure of that. In a duel, properly conducted, you would at least have some chance of survival.'

The uneasiness in Moncade's eyes escalated into alarm. He would have heard of the Comte de Bouttin's reputation for violent anger and for reckless courage. During his service with the Duc de Narbonne, he would have seen the wild bravado and extravagant behaviour of which the young bloods of society were capable.

'This is madness! I have done nothing and yet you would murder me!'

'Why do you persist in denying the part you played in our duel?' Gautier asked him.

'I know nothing of it, I tell you!' Moncade repeated.

'We can prove that you did. Everything here today is exactly as it was when the comte and I fought. Our seconds are the same.' Gautier pointed towards the other group of men who stood watching from a distance. 'So is the doctor. Monsieur Raspail is here and so is the man who called himself Fosse.'

'That isn't him,' Moncade blurted out. Then, as he realized what he had said, he turned pale.

'How do you know?' Gautier asked him at once. 'You said you knew nothing about our duel.'

'That's enough for me,' the Comte de Bouttin declared. 'He has confessed. Let us get on with the business.' He turned and called out to his seconds, 'Gentlemen, bring us the pistols.'

'Wait,' Gautier said. 'Although he planned our duel, it could not have been he who conceived the whole plot. After all, why should he have wished to harm me or you? No, someone else must have been behind it.'

'In that case, he is the one I shall fight.'

'Why not tell us who gave you your orders?' Gautier asked Moncade. 'Who was it who thought of the plan and provided the money to pay the Comte de Bouttin and Fosse?'

Moncade did not reply but stared in front of him sullenly. Surat had not given him time to dress properly when he arrested him and he was wearing neither a top coat nor a hat. Small beads of sweat had formed along his upper lip and on his temple and his bald skull glistened.

'He's not going to tell us,' the comte said impatiently. 'We'll waste no more time. Give me the pistols.'

Raspail, who was holding the box of duelling pistols, came towards them as the comte beckoned to him. The alarm which Moncade had been struggling to control began slipping into panic. Physical courage had not been one of the qualities required in a footman working for a wealthy household, nor had he needed it as a proprietor of a small hotel.

'Can't you understand?' He was shouting now. 'There is nothing to tell!'

The comte took the pistols from the box and held one in each hand as though he were weighing them against each other. Then he handed one to Raspail. 'Give this one to the wretch.'

Turning from Moncade, he walked away, counting his paces aloud as he might in a duel. Raspail held the other pistol out to Moncade who brushed it away fearfully. The comte had stopped and turned now and was facing him, holding his pistol at arm's length as though ready to fire.

'Wait!' Moncade shouted hysterically. 'Don't fire! For pity's sake don't shoot!'

His words were still hanging in the damp morning air when they were cut short by the sound of a shot. The report echoed through the Bois, exactly as the explosion of the comte's pistol had in the first duel and the birds in the trees flew up in alarm. Once again Gautier had the feeling that he was watching a scene being replayed, history repeating itself in a bright cameo of violence. Instinctively he looked towards the Comte de Bouttin, but this time his pistol had not exploded and he stood there, staring in astonishment. Following the line of his stare, Gautier saw that it was Moncade who had fallen. He lay on the ground, clutching at the left side of his chest and screaming with pain.

Almost immediately the doctor was beside him, kneeling down, pulling his hands away, so that he could examine the wound from which blood was beginning to spurt.

'Why did you fire?' Duthrey called out to the comte reproachfully. 'He did not even have a pistol.'

'I never fired.'

'Nor did I,' Raspail said, holding out the pistol which he had been offering to Moncade.

'Then who did?'

'I think you will find the answer there,' Marigny said.

He pointed towards the copse of trees from where Surat and the two policemen were emerging. Surat and one of the policemen were holding a prisoner between them, pinning his arms firmly to his side. The other policeman was carrying, by its barrel and at arm's length, a rifle. As they approached, Gautier saw that the prisoner was the Minister of Justice, François Godilot.

When the four men drew near, Godilot said to Gautier calmly, 'You are supposed to have some authority over this man Surat. Tell him to release me at once.'

'It was the minister who fired the rifle,' Surat explained. 'Then he tried to get away to a coupé which he had left standing waiting beyond those trees.'

'The man is an imbecile,' Godilot said contemptuously. 'I was coming here from my home, intending to stop you and the comte fighting another duel, when I heard a shot. A man was running away and he dropped that rifle. I picked it up, meaning to chase him, but before I could these fools grabbed me.'

'That isn't true,' Surat said stolidly. 'I saw him fire the rifle.'

Gautier glanced quickly towards Moncade who lay on the ground, no longer writhing nor moaning, but motionless. He wondered whether the man had fainted with pain and whether the Minister of Justice might be assuming he was dead. For Moncade to be shot was an eventuality which he had never even considered and now he would have to improvise.

He thought he could see a way of turning the situation to his advantage, but the ill-timing which had already disrupted his plan prevented him from doing what he had in mind. Hearing the sound of horses' hooves, he looked round and saw a carriage draw up a short distance from them. The Prefect of Police got out, properly dressed and accompanied by the Director-General of the Sûreté.

'Thank Heavens you have come,' Godilot told Courtrand. 'Your men here have gone insane.'

'What is this?' Courtrand stared in horror at the sight of a government minister being held by two policemen.

'The minister has just shot this man,' Gautier replied, pointing towards Moncade.

'I did nothing of the kind.' Godilot pointed towards Surat. 'That imbecile jumped to the conclusion that I had.'

'Release the minister at once!' Courtrand ordered.

'Might it not be better if we first established what really did happen?' Gautier asked.

'This is all your doing, Gautier. It has the unmistakable style of your handiwork. This time you have gone too far. For an officer under suspension to behave in this way is monstrous!'

'Gautier's suspension was lifted by me,' the Prefect of Police said quietly.

Gautier glanced at him, but only briefly. Then he crossed to where Moncade was lying. 'Perhaps there is a way of resolving this matter, Messieurs,' he said and then added to the doctor, 'I shall have to ask your patient some questions.'

'All right, but be brief. I believe the bullet has penetrated his lung.'

Moncade was still conscious, his face rigid in a grimace of pain and he was breathing with difficulty, seeming to struggle for air. When Gautier bent over him and called his name, he opened his eyes. He gasped, 'I was unarmed—had no weapon and yet the comte shot me!' His time as a servant in the Duc de Narbonne's household had filled him with a staunch belief in the chivalry of the aristocracy. He repeated, 'How could he have fired?'

'It was not the Comte de Bouttin who shot you. His pistol is still undischarged.' Gautier pointed at the rifle which the policeman was holding. 'You were shot with a rifle from a distance by someone hiding in those trees.'

'Who did it?'

'Can you not see anyone here who might have pulled the trigger?'

Moncade looked up at the people gathered around him. Everyone was there by this time: the comte and his seconds, the doctor, Duthrey, Marigny, Madame de Nyren, the Minister of Justice, the prefect and Courtrand. Slowly and painfully Moncade turned his head to let his stare move round the circle of people. It rested on each one of them in turn, but his expression never changed and Gautier could only admire his self-control.

'Is there no one here who would have wished to silence you?' he asked Moncade.

'Silence me? Why?'

'To stop you implicating him.'

Moncade managed a twisted smile. 'Implicating him in what? Taking money from a woman who is dead?'

'No, that was your idea alone. I mean implicating him in the murder of Lady Dorothy Strathy, in attempting to murder the Comte de Bouttin and myself, in the poisoning of Jean-Jacques Touraine.'

'Are you saying that this man was responsible for all those crimes?' Courtrand asked incredulously.

Ignoring the interruption, Gautier looked at Moncade steadily. 'Whoever it was who fired the shot tried to kill you to save himself,' he said. 'Knowing that, are you ready to go to the guillotine alone?'

The reference to the guillotine shattered Moncade just as Gautier hoped it would. The word was one which conjured up an image that always lurked in the mind's recesses of those who lived by crime:

the stumbling walk between two warders across the cobbled square in front of the prison at La Roquette, the knife blade suspended high, glinting in the last of the night's moonlight, the snap of the rope that held it up and the deadly hiss of its shimmering plunge to the bare neck below. The terror which the image evoked was too much for Moncade.

'No!' he screamed, 'I didn't kill the English woman. He made me do it! And arranged the duel. Touraine too. It was all his idea!'

Still clutching at his chest with his left hand, he pointed accusingly with his right at the Minister of Justice. Godilot's mouth tightened but he said nothing. Moncade went on, 'Why shouldn't I tell them? You were ready to kill me to save yourself.'

'Hold your tongue, you fool!' Godilot said roughly. 'Can't you see he is tricking you into confessing? He has no proof for all these accusations.'

'But why were you going to kill me?' Moncade demanded hysterically, panting as he fought for breath. 'I would never have betrayed you.'

'No,' Gautier agreed. 'You kept his secret for ten years; his secret and yours.'

'What secret?' Courtrand asked impatiently. The events he was watching had passed beyond his comprehension.

'The minister was the third man in the Flower Girl Affair, and Moncade the man who procured the girls.'

Nobody spoke. Everyone in the group stared at Gautier and then slowly, reluctantly, shifted their gaze to the Minister of Justice. Their silence, shocked and bewildered, was more damning than any spoken accusation.

'You tried to kill me!' Moncade said, whimpering now.

Godilot looked at him with contempt. 'I wish I had!'

19

THE BOAT TRAIN for Calais was due to leave in twenty minutes. It stood in the Gare du Nord with steam hissing up below the carriages, as though impatient to be gone, its passengers watching anxiously while porters loaded their luggage into the compartments. Three children, two girls with their hair in long plaits and their brother in a sailor suit, chased each other around excitedly, ignoring the reprimands of their governess. The stationmaster, in frock coat and top hat, stood watching them tolerantly.

'In a few hours you will be home, Mademoiselle,' the Prefect of Police said. 'Do we always appreciate the marvels of modern travel, I wonder?'

'I am sorry to be leaving Paris,' Miss Newbolt replied. 'Truly I am.'

'In spite of everything you have endured, being cross-examined by the police, arrested, held in prison?'

'It was an adventure.' Miss Newbolt smiled at Gautier meaningfully as she added, 'And I had wonderful experiences, never to be forgotten.'

The embarrassment Gautier felt at her remark was, he supposed, not dissimilar to that which the prefect must have experienced when he found Gautier at Madame de Nyren's soirée, but the prefect showed his diplomacy by not even glancing at him after Miss Newbolt had spoken. The two of them had gone to the Gare du Nord to see her leave and they were strolling up and down the platform by the waiting train. Miss Newbolt was wearing a new dress, purchased no doubt out of the compensation she had been paid by the government, and a hat with an extravagant display of ostrich feathers. Although it was scarcely needed as protection against a weak, watery sun, she was also carrying a parasol.

‘I hope at least, Mademoiselle, that you are not leaving with too bad an impression of the French police,’ the prefect said.

‘Bad? How could I? You not only found the murderers of Lady Dorothy and poor Monsieur Touraine, but you have destroyed what might have permanently damaged the whole fabric of French justice, a corrupt minister.’

‘Not to mention the murderers of the wretched Mateer.’

‘One crime led to another, did it not?’

‘That often happens,’ Gautier remarked. ‘Crime drags the perpetrator down in a vicious spiral until he is finally trapped at the bottom and pays the price.’

‘Why do you suppose they murdered Lady Dorothy? Was she really a threat to them?’

‘Probably not,’ Gautier replied. ‘The enquiries she was making into her brother’s past would not have uncovered the part that Godilot and Moncade played in the Flower Girl Affair, although she might well have found out that Simone Decartier was dead and that Moncade had been taking the money intended for her.’

‘Such a trifling amount!’

‘Yes and even if Lady Dorothy had found out he had been stealing the money, she would almost certainly have done nothing about it, for fear of stirring up a scandal. But when you arrived at his hotel talking about letters the earl had written to Rosebud, Moncade took fright. He knew about the earl’s meetings with the girl and had no idea of what she might have told him or what might be in his letters. So he contacted Godilot and they worked out a plan to have Lady Dorothy murdered in such a way that you would be the natural suspect.’

Part of the plan, Gautier explained, was that once Miss Newbolt came under suspicion, the Minister of Justice would be able to get his hands on the earl’s letters. She would be searched and so would her room at the Hotel Cheltenham. They had not anticipated that she would lock the letters away in the hotel safe deposit. Then, unfortunately for him, Touraine had found the letters.

‘There must have been something in one of them which implicated Godilot in the Flower Girl Affair and Touraine took them to his friend Moncade suggesting they might blackmail the minister. He didn’t know Moncade himself had been involved.’

Gautier turned to Miss Newbolt. 'I suppose Touraine came to see you in prison?'

'Yes. He was most sympathetic. We had a long chat.'

'Their plan was astute,' the prefect remarked. 'Why should anyone suppose that the Minister of Justice and an obscure hotel keeper should wish to have a titled Englishwoman killed?'

'What I can't understand,' Miss Newbolt said to Gautier, 'is why they decided that you also must be killed.'

'The minister lost his head when he learned that I had found the cigarette case which Simone had given the earl. He feared I would guess the significance of the rosebud which was engraved on it.'

'But what would that have told you? That the earl had been infatuated with one of the girls in the affair. Nothing more. You would not know about the earl's letters.'

'You don't know our Inspector Gautier,' the prefect told Miss Newbolt, smiling. 'He has a reputation for brilliance, for having an almost supernatural flair for unravelling even the most complex crimes.'

'I'm not at all surprised.'

'As you said, one crime led to another. Mateer, who had been hired to kill Lady Dorothy had to be murdered himself because he had put the whole plan in jeopardy by stealing her jewellery.'

They had been walking up the platform but stopped before they reached the locomotive, fearing what its hissing steam and soot might do to Miss Newbolt's new dress and parasol. As they were turning round, the stationmaster came up and told them the train would be 15 minutes late in leaving. A small technical fault was the reason, he explained to the prefect apologetically, minor damage to a coupling which was even then being repaired. The prefect pulled out his pocket watch.

'I am desolate, Mademoiselle,' he told Miss Newbolt, 'but I shall not be able to stay until your train carries you away from us. The Minister for the Interior is expecting me.'

'Of course, Monsieur. I understand.'

'There is one question I would like to ask you if I may, Monsieur le Préfet,' Gautier said. 'In the Bois you told the Director-General that you had lifted my suspension.'

'Yes, it was untrue.' The prefect smiled. 'But only a small lie, you'll agree. I wished to hear your explanation of why the minister had been arrested.'

'Does that mean you suspected him?'

'Not of having Lady Dorothy murdered, but I have always believed that there had been a third man in the Flower Girl Affair, a rich and powerful man.'

The third man, the prefect explained, would have had to be wealthy. To have kept his name out of the court case would have meant buying the silence of at the very least the three girls; a dowry was the price he had paid to make Simone change her mind and her testimony and the other two girls would have expected no less. Probably others would have had to be bought, the concierge of the apartment building, perhaps, and maybe one or two policemen. He could have relied on the Duc de Caramond and Charles Bailly not to betray him, through loyalty and a sense of honour, but it would have needed influence to make sure that the Advocate General did not have any awkward questions asked in court.

'And Godilot was a lawyer.'

'With lawyer friends. The legal profession looks after its own.'

'He must have been very fearful of being exposed to have gone to such lengths,' Miss Newbolt remarked.

'He stood to lose everything: his wife, his wife's money, his ministerial position. And more than that. Many people believed Godilot would have been the next Prime Minister.'

'And now he has lost it all.'

'Yes,' the prefect agreed. 'Once again, Gautier, you have brought matters to a satisfactory conclusion. But I have to say that the way you did it, the pretended duel, the gallery of people in the Bois, was very bizarre.'

'It was, I know. A most unlikely plan which was fortunate to end well. But I had no alternative. Suspended from duty as I was, I could think of no other way of bringing Godilot and Moncade face to face in circumstances when one might incriminate the other.'

'I suppose you are saying that we must take care not to suspend you ever again.' The prefect laughed and turned to Miss Newbolt. 'And now, alas, Mademoiselle, I am obliged to leave you.'

'Goodbye, Monsieur, and thank you again for your kindness and courtesy.'

'Paris will be a sadder place without you.'

Miss Newbolt held out her hand for the prefect to kiss, instinctively, like a woman who was accustomed to receiving the devotion of men. Gautier remembered the quiet, self-effacing lady's companion whom he had met in the Hotel Cheltenham not so many days ago. The change in Miss Newbolt had been remarkable. She looked not only happy and self-assured but radiant, not a moth any longer but a butterfly, bright and eager. After the prefect had left them they turned and walked back along the platform towards the carriage in which she would be travelling.

'You must be very pleased with yourself, Jean-Paul,' she teased Gautier. 'It is a pity I shall not be here to prevent success turning your head.'

'There's no danger of that. I realize only too well that I mishandled the investigation into Lady Dorothy's murder.'

'In what way?'

'I should never have allowed myself to become involved in a duel.'

Miss Newbolt laid a hand on Gautier's arm. 'You were distraught after your wife's death.'

'Her death may have been the cause of my stupidity but it does not excuse it.'

Since the Comte de Bouttin's pistol had exploded, Gautier had often tried to analyse his motives for accepting the challenge to fight the duel. Suzanne's death had certainly affected his judgement but he believed there were other, less creditable reasons for his behaviour. Had the success he had enjoyed in solving difficult and often spectacular crimes, the reputation he had made for himself and the esteem in which he was held by his friends at the Café Corneille, pushed him into believing that he now had a place in Paris society and should conform to its mores? He was not certain of the answer.

'If I had used orthodox police procedure in investigating Lady Dorothy's death I believe I should have solved the crime much earlier.'

'What should you have done?'

'When we knew Lady Dorothy's jewellery had been stolen, a squad of men should have been sent to visit the pawnshops. That might well have led us to Mateer before he was murdered. And I should have brought Moncade and Touraine to the Sûreté and interrogated them severely to find out what they knew.'

What Gautier meant was that he should have questioned the two men in the way some other officers from the Sûreté would have done, a way that bordered on violence and which on occasions slipped over that border. It was a practice which Courtrand was willing to condone but one which Gautier would never adopt, in spite of what he was now saying.

'And me as well,' Miss Newbolt said. 'The lies I told cannot have helped. I'm sorry.'

Gautier smiled. She was right but nothing would be gained by rebuking her now and he understood the motives for her lies. He said, 'In any event, I should have realized much sooner than I did that the Minister of Justice must be in some way involved.'

'I don't see why.'

'Only Godilot knew about the cigarette case inscribed with the rosebud which I had found in Lady Dorothy's suite. I mentioned it in the first report that I wrote on the murder but never again subsequently since it did not appear to have any relevance. Only the minister saw that report. It was sent directly to him as the Prefect of Police was not in Paris.'

'Do you think he realized its significance?'

'Without a doubt. He would have known that the Earl of Tain had been in Paris during the Flower Girl trial and that he had become infatuated with the girl Rosebud. He must have feared that I would have found out about that as well, that I would start delving into the past and that the whole affair would be opened up again.'

'So you were tricked into fighting a duel in which you would be maimed or killed?'

'Exactly.'

Miss Newbolt sighed and shook her head, as though she found difficulty in believing that anyone could be capable of the kind of villainy which Gautier had described. 'I am sure that what you say is true,' she said, 'and yet I find myself feeling sorry for Monsieur Godilot. He has great charm.'

She was right. François Godilot had ample charm and it had been at the same time his strength and his undoing. And yet if he had trusted to his charm, if instead of trying to conceal his part in the Flower Girl Affair he had faced trial, he might have escaped with a light sentence or even no sentence at all. With his eloquence and his charm he would have won the sympathy of many people who thought the girls in the case had only themselves to blame, who might have admired his boldness and honesty. Instead, he had been too cowardly or too greedy to put his trust in his charm and now he would get his reward under the blade of the guillotine.

'What will you do when you reach home?' Gautier asked Miss Newbolt. It was not an occasion to be talking of crime and degradation and seeing her happiness, he wished to share it.

'I don't think I shall ever be a lady's companion again.'

'I should hope not! You have too independent a spirit, too good a mind.'

'Thank you.'

Gautier could not help noticing that now she accepted as her due a compliment which would probably have made her blush with embarrassment not many days previously. She smiled as she told him, 'I have a secret which I shall confide in you, Jean-Paul. Back at home there is a man living not far from us whom I have always admired. He is a gentleman farmer and a year ago he had the misfortune to lose his wife. He has three young children and so one may suppose that before long he will be looking for a second wife to be a mother to them.'

Miss Newbolt paused before she added, 'Perhaps that is no more than conceit, but I cannot help hoping that when I return home my gentleman farmer may see me filling that role.'

Listening to her, watching her, Gautier was certain she was right. The farmer and other men too would see Miss Newbolt in a new light when she returned home, not on account of her new clothes and her changed manner, but because her spirit and her dignity had been tempered by an experience which would have destroyed many women. She would marry now and he was pleased for her. At the same time his pleasure was lessened by a sadness at the knowledge that she was moving irrevocably out of his life. He had no wish to hold on to her, to keep her for himself, he felt no desire for her, but she was passing out of his life as so many other women had and it saddened him.

Along the platform the guard blew his whistle and the passengers began boarding the train. Miss Newbolt kissed him lightly on the lips. He watched her climb up from the platform and take her place in her compartment. But suddenly he knew he could not bear to watch her leave and, after nodding at her as she waved to him, he turned abruptly and walked away down the platform.